ACCIDENTALLY MATCHED

CATHRYN BROWN

Sienna Bay Press

PO Box 158582

Nashville, Tennessee 37215

www.cathrynbrown.com

Cover designed by Najla Qamber Designs

(www.najlaqamberdesigns.com)

Publisher's Note: This is a work of fiction. Names, characters, places, and incidents are a product of the author's imagination. Locales and public names are sometimes used for atmospheric purposes. Any resemblance to actual people, living or dead, or to businesses, companies, events, or institutions is completely coincidental.

Accidentally Matched/Cathryn Brown. - 1st ed.

ISBN: 978-1-945527-31-9

❀ Created with Vellum

DEAR READER

I hope you enjoy Noah and Rachel's story, the first book in the Alaska Matchmakers Romance series. I could see the first part of this book in my head for two years before I wrote it. I'm glad to finally be able to share it with you.

In *Accidentally Matched*, there's adventure in the Alaska wilderness, small town charm, and big city moments. Or I should say, a big city when you're an Alaskan. Anchorage, the largest city in the state, is more than a thousand miles from Seattle, Washington, so it's *the* big city.

I was once in Talkeetna about this time of year. We took a boat up a large river there and big pieces of ice like mini icebergs were floating in the water. As I did, Rachel and Noah might wish they'd been in that part of Alaska later in the year.

Noah's mother is the matchmaker that introduces the two of them. You'll have to keep reading to see if she's the only matchmaker . . .

CHAPTER ONE

*R*achel Fitzpatrick leaned against the small airline's counter. "I can't get to Talkeetna today?"

A man with a full head of gray hair and weathered skin stared at her. "No, miss. As I said, we have no available pilots right now to fly you to Talkeetna." He gave her a satisfied nod, as though he knew he had communicated the facts in a way that she would finally understand.

"I had a reservation."

"For yesterday. That pilot is out on a different run right now. He won't be back until late."

One flight delay had led to an overnight stay in Seattle, and here she stood. "I had hoped the reservation would move me higher on the list."

He shrugged. "Not when everyone's out on other runs."

"Is there a bus?"

"There is."

"Perfect! Where do I catch it?"

"Downtown. But it's only during the summer months. There's a train too."

counter. Since no one else was in the place, she called out to him, "You know that he's a good pilot?"

"None better. He'll get you where you're wanting to go."

The woman patted Rachel on the arm. "Noah is my son. But I have a favor to ask of you."

Oh, so she *was* matchmaking. Rachel wouldn't go out with her son even if he did seem to offer the only access to Talkeetna today.

But Anita's next words surprised her. "I'd like your help in playing a small joke on him." The woman raised her eyebrows and grinned.

Not a date then. "What kind of favor?"

"Your name made me think of it. Can you do an Irish accent?"

Rachel leaned back and looked the lady over. This must be the strangest request from a mother. Ever. But if it was the ticket to Talkeetna and David, why not?

She shrugged. "My dad's side of the family is from Ireland. I've been there quite a few times. Yes, I can do a better than average Irish accent."

Anita grinned. "Excellent. Watch his expression when you meet him. Then maintain that accent the whole time."

"He won't be upset when he finds out, will he?"

"Not a chance. All of my boys love a practical joke. Besides, he'll never know. You get on and off the plane as an Irishwoman. I'll tell him later." She rubbed her hands together with glee.

Rachel laughed.

"He's at his plane now. I can run you over there, or you can walk to it in about ten minutes."

Rachel felt the weight of her journey and the amount of time it had taken her to get there. Anita seemed nice, and she

CHAPTER ONE

*R*achel Fitzpatrick leaned against the small airline's counter. "I can't get to Talkeetna today?"

A man with a full head of gray hair and weathered skin stared at her. "No, miss. As I said, we have no available pilots right now to fly you to Talkeetna." He gave her a satisfied nod, as though he knew he had communicated the facts in a way that she would finally understand.

"I had a reservation."

"For yesterday. That pilot is out on a different run right now. He won't be back until late."

One flight delay had led to an overnight stay in Seattle, and here she stood. "I had hoped the reservation would move me higher on the list."

He shrugged. "Not when everyone's out on other runs."

"Is there a bus?"

"There is."

"Perfect! Where do I catch it?"

"Downtown. But it's only during the summer months. There's a train too."

As excitement grew again, she tamped it down. "Only in the summer?"

"It occasionally runs in the winter. It will be close to a week before its next trip to Talkeetna. You could drive."

Polite as she preferred to be, even she couldn't hold back a groan. "I haven't driven in years. There isn't a whole lot of need for a car when I live and work in Arlington, Virginia."

The man nodded, but in a hesitant way, making her wonder if he knew where Arlington was.

"That's just outside of Washington, D.C," she explained.

"Ahh. Well, I'm sorry, miss. I can't help you."

Rachel wandered over to one of two chairs pushed against the wall, apparently their waiting area. It seemed it wasn't easy to get to Talkeetna. She wished her brother hadn't found a way.

The man at the counter waved at someone behind her, so Rachel turned to see who. A woman about her mother's age had entered the hangar. The woman's forest-green sweater had a pattern of daisies woven into it, and her purse had a bouquet of flowers embroidered on the navy fabric.

As Rachel turned to walk out of the hangar, hoping to find a hotel near the airport—one that would have a shuttle service—she passed the woman.

"I love all the flowers." Rachel gestured at the sweater and purse.

The woman stopped. "Excuse me?"

Her startled tone assured Rachel that she had offended the only Alaskan she'd spoken to other than the man at the counter. As she opened her mouth to apologize, the woman interrupted.

"You *like* my flowers?"

"They're cheerful. And I can use some cheer right about now."

"My family does *not* love my flowers. I'm Anita." The woman extended her hand for a handshake. "Anita O'Connell."

"Rachel Fitzpatrick." Rachel shook her hand. Expecting that to be the end of it, she turned once again toward the door.

"Do you need directions?"

Rachel stopped and faced the woman. "Only if you can tell me how to walk to Talkeetna this afternoon."

"That isn't going to happen. It's about a two-hour drive." The woman looked her over, seeming to take her measure. "Are you going to meet your boyfriend in Talkeetna?"

Rachel laughed. "No. My brother."

The woman nodded slowly. "I imagine you're in a hurry, though, to get back home to your boyfriend."

Was the woman fishing for information? The last thing she wanted in her life was a matchmaker, but she didn't have it in her to lie. "I'm not dating anyone."

The woman's smile grew broader. "I may have a flight solution for you. Let me talk to Amos over there and see if he's thought of this."

Anita marched up to the counter, and after a brief conversation with Amos, they both turned toward her and grinned, which unnerved her. Then Anita pulled out her cell phone and made a call. Sliding her phone back into her flowered purse, the woman marched back to Rachel.

"We found you a ride to Talkeetna, and it's leaving in about half an hour." Anita handed her a piece of paper that had a series of letters and numbers on it and a man's name— Noah. Rachel looked from the paper to the man behind the counter. Since no one else was in the place, she called out to him, "You know that he's a good pilot?"

"None better. He'll get you where you're wanting to go."

The woman patted Rachel on the arm. "Noah is my son. But I have a favor to ask of you."

Oh, so she *was* matchmaking. Rachel wouldn't go out with her son even if he did seem to offer the only access to Talkeetna today.

But Anita's next words surprised her. "I'd like your help in playing a small joke on him." The woman raised her eyebrows and grinned.

Not a date then. "What kind of favor?"

"Your name made me think of it. Can you do an Irish accent?"

Rachel leaned back and looked the lady over. This must be the strangest request from a mother. Ever. But if it was the ticket to Talkeetna and David, why not?

She shrugged. "My dad's side of the family is from Ireland. I've been there quite a few times. Yes, I can do a better than average Irish accent."

Anita grinned. "Excellent. Watch his expression when you meet him. Then maintain that accent the whole time."

"He won't be upset when he finds out, will he?"

"Not a chance. All of my boys love a practical joke. Besides, he'll never know. You get on and off the plane as an Irishwoman. I'll tell him later." She rubbed her hands together with glee.

Rachel laughed.

"He's at his plane now. I can run you over there, or you can walk to it in about ten minutes."

Rachel felt the weight of her journey and the amount of time it had taken her to get there. Anita seemed nice, and she appeared to know the owner of this charter company well, so she would trust her. "A ride would be great, thank you."

Noah stared at the phone in his hand and sighed. Then he put it back into his pocket. Family got him to do things he wouldn't do for anyone else. He had brought his mother into Anchorage for a larger city shopping trip, and she planned to take a commercial flight home tomorrow with her purchases. But now she wanted him to give a ride to some woman who appreciated her flowers. He knew from experience that rarely happened.

When a woman chose to dress in floral from head to toe and decorate everything she could get her hands on with flowers—well, everything her husband and five sons would allow—it took a special someone to appreciate that. In his experience, that special someone was usually in his grandmother's age group. Which wasn't an insult to anyone that age, but extensive flowers seemed to appeal to them more than they did to a twenty-something.

He stowed his backpack on one side of the backseat and moved his ice chest to the floor to make room for his passenger. After closing that door, he went around to the other side of the plane to double-check that Zeke, his Belgian shepherd, was securely strapped in.

"Are you excited about our trip, boy?" He took Zeke's panting and the lick he swiped across his cheek as an affirmative. His dog liked nothing better than running down trails, jumping in streams, and stopping to sniff the air to see if he could find any other animals on it. Throw in a dog treat every now and again, and he was in doggie heaven.

Out of the corner of his eye, he saw his mother's white rental car pull up in front of his plane. When he turned to the car, and the passenger door opened, he knew he'd miscalculated. Somehow, his mother had actually found a woman his age who liked flowers, a pretty redhead who had a city look to her.

His mother walked over, the younger woman following. "Noah, I'd like you to meet Rachel."

Rachel extended her hand to him. "I'm pleased to be meeting you."

Noah froze. "You're Irish?"

The woman hesitated, seeming not to know what to do with her hand. Noah shook it as she smiled hesitantly and replied, "Aye."

His gaze shot to his mother, who stared at him with a smirk on her face. She knew his soft spot for Irish accents. His grandmother had come from there, and he had many happy childhood memories surrounding her. Even when visiting her now as an adult, he more than any of his brothers loved listening to her voice and the lilt of her accent.

Noah blinked and studied the woman in front of him. Her red hair was pulled up in a bun on top of her head, not one of those newer style messy buns, but a tight, almost Victorian bun. She had dressed appropriately for Alaska in a heavy jacket with a sweater peeking out at the neck, jeans, and sneakers. All appeared brand-new.

"Well, if everything is set, I'll leave you two to get going on your flight."

Noah's gaze turned to his mother, and he narrowed his eyes. She was matchmaking again.

She had the nerve to grin at him. "There aren't any problems, are there, Noah?"

If he refused to take this woman to Talkeetna, the direction he was flying anyway, it would be mean. His mother knew he didn't have that in him. He'd been played by the master. "I think you've done all you need to, Mom."

She gave him a small wave with her fingers and said, "I hope so. I truly hope so."

He and Rachel watched his mother's car drive off. Then they turned to each other.

Rachel spoke before he had a chance. "I appreciate your flying me to Talkeetna. But I don't want to be a bother to anyone. Please tell me if I need to find a different way to get there."

Okay. So he was the jerk of the hour. "It's no problem. I'll make a short stop to drop you off there and then continue on. I'm going fishing and camping in that general area for a week." He smiled to reassure her, and she smiled back.

"I've never been in an airplane this small. Not even close. It looks too small to fly."

He laughed. "This Cessna 170 is closer to the size of a bird than a 747 and birds fly well. It's safe and also fun to fly."

As he settled Rachel into her seat, he saw Zeke leaning forward to catch her scent, but Rachel didn't seem to notice. His dog must have approved, because if he hadn't, he would have barked up a storm. That was one point in his mother's favor.

Rachel fidgeted nervously as he climbed into his seat and put on his seatbelt and headset. While he went through the preflight checklist he'd committed to memory, she quietly said, "The man from the charter service said that you knew how to fly well."

Noah laughed. "I learned to fly as soon as I could. I've

logged many hours in the air and flown in weather that you can't even begin to imagine, in both civilian and military planes. That experience is what got me my job as an airline pilot."

Rachel swiveled toward him. "That's your job? I've never known anyone who flew for a living."

In spite of his annoyance with his mother, Rachel's accent made him smile. "I'm never happier than when I'm sitting in an airplane soaring through the air." He clapped his mouth shut, realizing he'd given away too much of himself to a woman he had just met.

She settled back into the seat. "I'm glad to hear it."

Rachel sat up straight and stiff when he called "Clear!" out the window and then started the plane. With the prop spinning, he taxied over to the edge of the runway and requested permission to take off. When they rolled onto the runway, Rachel's handwringing returned.

"Don't worry. We'll be in the air soon."

"If your words are intended to reassure me, you've missed the mark. I don't like to fly."

Noah grinned. His mother had gotten this completely wrong. She needed to add "love of flying" to her list of matchmaking requirements. Feeling set free from any expectations of his mother, he pulled onto the runway.

Noah was handsome when he smiled, but she wouldn't let that thought go any further. She had one reason for coming to Alaska. She had to stay focused.

The plane moved faster and faster and faster down the runway until it lifted off, exactly as a large plane would, but it felt somehow more real when the runway and the sky were inches away from her. The plane climbed up into the clouds, white swirling around them, then it popped above them and into sunshine.

"Wow! The sun is shining!"

Noah laughed. "The sun is always shining. Sometimes you have to get beyond the clouds."

She turned toward him. "Is that a quote from someone?"

"Noah O'Connell."

An odd sound came from the backseat, almost a whimper.

"What was that?"

Noah pointed to her right. "Grab a treat out of that bag and hold it over the top of the seat."

Rachel picked up the bag he'd pointed to and found it filled with bone-shaped treats. When she held one in the air over the seat, she was awarded with a lick on her hand as it was scooped off and then a soft woof. She sat back in her seat with her hand on her chest. "You have a dog back there?"

"He goes everywhere with me."

Great. She was sitting in a small airplane with a stranger, a handsome one she'd admit, and a dog. She had zero knowledge of dogs. Her parents hadn't allowed them to have pets.

They crossed over a saltwater inlet. On the other side, trees and small lakes and rivers filled the landscape. "This is beautiful." And it was. Even the green fields of the Irish countryside, broken by rock walls and sheep which always seemed to quiet her soul, were nothing like this openness. Thinking about Ireland reminded her that she currently had an Irish accent. She hoped she would easily find David in Talkeetna and that he appreciated her efforts. She sighed. "It's raw beauty untouched by man."

Noah turned to look at her and gave her a long stare. "It's why I live in Alaska. It's why I fly. I tried living outside, but I missed this." He gestured to the view out his window.

"Outside? You lived in a tent?"

He laughed. "Outside with a capital O. That's what Alaskans call the rest of the country."

She laughed too. "I guess I'm a greenhorn."

"Alaskans might say you're a Cheechako. That's someone who's new here. We'll just call you a newcomer or visitor."

"Let's go with newcomer. I may need to visit again." She stared out the window, watching nature roll by under the plane. "I never asked. How long of a flight is it from Anchorage to Talkeetna?"

"Depending on headwinds and tailwinds and everything else, probably about thirty or forty minutes."

She smiled broadly. "Then I'll get to see David soon. I can't wait to give him a big hug."

They flew in silence for a few minutes. "Those are popular fishing rivers that we're flying over, the Big and Little Susitna. Up ahead is an old mining area I'm planning to explore someday. Petersville."

"It sounds like a lovely name for a town."

"I don't think it was ever considered a town. More a cluster of buildings whose inhabitants had the common goal of finding as much gold in the ground as they could. And they found a lot of it. They're still finding it today."

Something white poked through the cloud layer ahead of them. "What's that?"

He looked to where she was pointing. "That is the top of the highest mountain in North America. Mt. McKinley. You may know of it as Denali. A lot of Alaskans still think of it as Mt. McKinley."

"It's beautiful. I'd like to see the whole mountain."

"Those are the days we all love, when the mountain is clear. You can even see it from Anchorage then."

She hoped the clouds cleared while she was here. "Have you ever thought about climbing the mountain?"

He shook his head. "I'm a flier, not a mountain climber. Someone I grew up with was."

"Was?"

"He died up there. Not too long after high school."

She could imagine what his family must have felt when a child died so young. "What a sad story."

Noah's expression was both sad and determined. "It is, but it isn't. His family and his friends all knew that he died doing what he loved. It would be the same if something happened to me in an airplane. Flying is close to breathing to me."

"It would still be sad. That's how the bards write about love."

"English major?"

"Fashion."

"Are you a fashion designer?"

"No, I work in the family's clothing business."

The engine clunked. She'd never been in a small plane, but it didn't sound right.

She watched Noah as the expression on his face passed from curiosity to seriousness to concern. Whatever had happened to the plane wasn't good.

He pushed a button on his headset and spoke into the microphone. Then he checked the connections and spoke again, repeating his call. When no one seemed to answer, she realized the radio had gone out too.

They were alone.

CHAPTER TWO

"*R*achel, look out your window." Her pilot's serious tone ratcheted up her fear level. "We need somewhere level and clear. It would be much better if we did not go down in trees or water. I remember coming here once when I was a kid. There are a lot of old mines, so we may find what we need."

"We're crashing?" She put her hand on her chest as her heartbeat speeded up and panic hit her, worse than anything she had ever felt in her life.

"I hope we don't crash. Look for a level place. *Please.*"

His words brought her to life. She had to hold down her fear, or she wouldn't be useful. *Focus, Rachel.* She looked out the window, searching the land below. "All I see is green and blue. Lakes and rivers. You said we weren't too far out from Talkeetna. Can we make it there?"

He held onto the wheel of the plane with both hands, as though he was holding it back. From what, she didn't even want to guess. "We can't make it to Talkeetna, Rachel. I'm going to need somewhere to land *very* soon."

She turned back to the window as Noah struggled with the plane. He seemed to be fighting to keep them airborne, and even with that, the ground grew closer at an alarming rate. Was she on her way to an ugly death in Alaska?

A road appeared to the right of the plane. "Noah!" She pointed. "There's a road down there."

He steered the plane in that direction. The lower they dropped, the clearer it became. He looked up and around as if assessing their position. "This is a rural road, not a city road that is nicely graded and smooth. And I'm not sure how wide it's going to be once we get down there."

Rachel watched out the window. A long strip, mostly tan on a flat piece of land with no trees, appeared to the right. "Is that a runway to our left?"

Noah gave a rough laugh. "Finding a runway out here would be nothing short of miraculous." He once again fought with the plane, holding onto the heavy steering wheel as he turned them slightly in that direction. Then he gasped as he saw where she was pointing. "It's a miracle! You're right, that looks like a runway. Even if it's slightly overgrown, we're above the treeline here, so there shouldn't be anything too ugly in the way. Maybe just a little bit of scrub." He flipped a switch and said, "Hold on. We're going to land there."

Rachel sat silently, watching as Noah tugged and turned and maneuvered the plane until he had lined it up with the runway. Then they started a fast descent, faster than she would have ever expected, as he headed them straight for it.

"We're coming in fast, Rachel. I don't have any choice because I don't have an engine to make a second pass or circle around and come back to the runway. We have one shot at this, so hold on."

Rachel grabbed onto the seat, closed her eyes, and said a

silent prayer. Then she opened them, and in those few seconds, the ground had rushed toward them.

Noah touched down, first the rear wheels and then the back wheel as they raced down the gravel strip bouncing over bumps. Right when she thought they wouldn't stop before they ran out of runway, he applied the brakes, and they slowed and came to a complete stop.

She'd survived. She put her hand on her racing heart. "We made it!"

His hand still gripped the wheel tightly. "I have been through some rough stuff over the years. One time when I landed on a carrier in the Indian Ocean in high swells, I wondered if I was going to make it. But none of it compared to what we just did. Rachel, I want you to realize that this wasn't a *small* miracle."

Noah opened the door of the plane and stepped out, feeling shaky. They'd made it down. To wherever down was. Somewhere around Petersville, he would guess, but the number of miles it would take for them to find civilization was anybody's guess. He glanced over to Rachel. She did not look like she was used to roughing it in the wilds of Alaska.

He unfastened Zeke's harness, but like her, the dog stayed in his seat.

Rachel stared forward with a petrified expression on her face. Her already fair skin had lost all color. He went around and opened the door, helped her unbuckle, and gave her a hand so she could step out. When she wobbled as she stepped on the ground, he put his hands on her shoulders to steady her.

She wrapped her arms around him and hugged him tightly. "We survived! We're alive!" She held onto him for a minute. Then, seeming to realize how close they were, she stepped back, her face turning pink. "I'm sorry. I should not have hugged the pilot."

"It's always okay to hug the pilot." He gave her his best shot at a grin to try to lighten the moment. Then the sound of her words sank in. Sometime during the last ten minutes, Rachel had lost her Irish accent. "Is your name really Rachel?"

Her brow furrowed. "Of course that's my name. Why would you ask that?"

"Because when I met a woman named Rachel earlier today, she sounded like someone from the Emerald Isle. Care to explain?"

She shook her head. "Your mother said—"

"My mother? This is a practical joke?"

"She said 'all of my boys love a practical joke.' I think that's a direct quote."

Caught between laughter and the seriousness of their situation, he sat on the ground to get his bearings. "I can't believe she did this!"

Zeke jumped to the ground and ran to his master. "Are you okay, boy?" he asked, scratching the dog's head. He appeared every bit as scared as Noah and Rachel had been.

"Well, Rachel, wherever you're from—"

"Arlington, Virginia."

He acknowledged her words with a nod. "My mother got you into what may be the adventure of your lifetime."

Her look of panic emphasized her words. "My thinking exactly. If I ever see her again, I'm not sure if I'll thank her for the opportunity." A wisp of a smile appeared and then vanished.

A sense of humor at a time like this might be helpful. He rubbed Zeke behind his ears. "You stay here. Don't go running off while I take care of things."

Noah walked around the plane with Zeke at his heels. He apparently didn't want his owner out of his sight. A careful check showed no damage to the plane, not a scratch or dent.

Rachel's color had improved slightly. "But what made the plane stopped working?"

Noah shrugged. "I have no idea. No one could keep a plane in better shape than I do. But there are still variables I can't control. I've only owned her for a couple of months, but I made sure a mechanic went over her with a fine-toothed comb. I'm pretty sure I'll be able to get somebody in here to fix the engine, so I'll be able to fly it out."

She whirled around to face him. "But you said someone would come to help you fix the plane." She pulled out her phone.

"This is Alaska. No one knows we're here. And your phone won't work this far away from civilization. We landed in a place where there doesn't seem to be anything that even looks like a telephone line or a satellite dish. The radio is out. And I don't see a cabin or any other shelter." When he saw panic race across her face, he quickly added, "This runway is here for a reason, either for something now or something in the past. I think we'll find shelter for tonight not too far away."

Rachel straightened her shoulders and nodded once. "I can do this. This will be a great story to tell about my trip to Alaska."

Relief surged through Noah. For a second, he thought he

was going to have a hysterical passenger. Male or female, that would not be a good thing. He glanced around them. The sun was high in the sky right now, but it would be chilly after dark in early May.

"Let's get our gear and start walking. The good news is that I was planning to be out in the woods for a week, so I have a tent, a sleeping bag, and food. It may not be the food you want to eat . . ."

Rachel waved her hand to dismiss that thought. "I think I will eat almost anything right now. I'll consider it an exotic delicacy of Alaska."

Noah chuckled. "Let's see if you still agree with that once you've had freeze-dried chili mac."

She laughed.

Noah moved the front seat forward, then reached into the backseat to grab her suitcase. After handing it to her, he took out his backpack, setting it on the ground and placing the ice chest beside it. He put on the pack, cinched it around his waist and chest, and picked up the ice chest. Then he patted the plane on the side and said in a low voice that he hoped Rachel couldn't hear, "Don't worry. I'll be back for you."

When he looked over at Rachel, he saw her grinning and knew that his words had not been missed. "She's served me well for the last few months."

"She?"

"Ships. Airplanes. For some reason, they all seem to be female. Maybe it's because of the trouble they cause men and the ways that they make them happy at the same time."

She swatted at his arm.

"Which direction, Mr. Outdoorsman?" She gestured at the scene in front of them.

Noah shielded his hand as he looked up at the sun, then he turned in a circle. Mt. McKinley was barely visible through some heavy clouds, but that told him the direction that was north, which was not the direction to go because there was nothing even approaching civilization at the base of Mt. McKinley.

He pointed to what he hoped was the southwest. "I believe that any roads will lead in that direction, and that's where we'll find the highway that leads to Talkeetna. There should be a building of some sort near this runway. The brush has grown over sections, and it hasn't had much recent use, but it's too nice of a runway to be out here with nothing nearby. The question is whether or not that structure is still stable enough for us to spend the night there. It could have been built decades ago and abandoned. I didn't notice any buildings or anything else except nature as we were coming in to land, did you?"

Rachel shook her head. "I didn't. But I was focused on the runway, and it's possible that I would have missed it. Once I saw this, I knew that's where we were going."

"Fair enough. Let's see what we can find."

They walked about a quarter of a mile and found nothing that direction, so they turned around and followed the edge of the land over a hill. When he was about to stop looking and pitch his tent, he found what he wanted. "There! Through those trees."

CHAPTER THREE

*R*achel squinted in the sun. A little bit of something brown peeked out between the brush, and she could see blue beyond it, so maybe it was a cabin on a stream or lake. Noah started in that direction, going down the hill. She followed behind and shifted her purse higher on her shoulder and lifted the suitcase in her arms, already wishing she had packed lighter. The suitcase may have wheels, but they were for smooth city surfaces.

The cabin was further than it had appeared, but when they arrived, Rachel was pleasantly surprised. About the size of the living room in her condo, the building was made of round logs with white between them and had a solid sense of stability and strength, like it could last forever.

Noah asked her to wait while he walked around the cabin and checked it out. He returned minutes later. "This could have been built fifty years ago. But it has been used in recent years. The metal roof appears solid, and I found a propane tank with a tube running into the house. That means there's probably a stove." He went over and knocked on the front door.

"Are you actually expecting to find someone here?"

"Not this time of year." When no one answered the door, he tried the knob, but it was locked. "This is Alaska. You can take shelter in someone's cabin if you need it. I'll repay them for anything that we use or damage." He stepped a few feet over to one window, rubbed dirt off it, and cupped his hands to see through it. Frowning, he stepped back. "*If* we can get in."

Rachel walked over and felt along the top of the door trim, coming back with a key in her hand.

Noah stared at it. "And you knew that was there because?"

"It's where I would put it."

Rachel watched as Noah opened his pack and started pulling things out. She'd found herself in a strange situation with the vanishing accent. She didn't think she'd hurt his feelings, but his trust in her had probably lessened. She wasn't sure how to reverse the damage.

"We'll be fine here tonight," Noah said. "Tomorrow we'll keep going."

Rachel took in her surroundings. It might be a far cry from the lodge she'd been booked into for the night, but the small cabin had a peacefulness about it, a simplicity that her life often didn't have. There was a stove next to a couple of scuffed white cupboards and a small, beat-up, rectangular table with a mismatched chair at each end. The simplicity extended to the fact that there was one double bed in the corner of the room.

"Hmm. Noah, who gets the bed?"

He stood. "I don't know what tomorrow brings. I do know that I want to get a good night's sleep for whatever that is. I'm going to sleep on one side of the bed."

"So you aren't going to be a gentleman and give it to me?" Rachel asked with what she hoped was a very polite note to her voice.

He gave a wry laugh. "Rachel, I'm not feeling particularly chivalrous right now. I just want to sleep. And to figure out how to teach my mother not to bring me any more beautiful redheads with fake Irish accents."

He'd called her beautiful. For a moment, she saw only the handsome man in the room. Then she noticed his frown, and she knew she had hurt him when he'd learned she'd been part of the joke. He might think her beautiful, but he still didn't look happy to be stuck with her.

Right now, she wondered what she'd been thinking when she went along with his mother's practical joke. It had sounded fun at the time. She'd needed a ride here. Well, she'd needed a ride to Talkeetna. "I understand." She stared at the floor, which appeared very hard and perhaps not as clean as it could have been. Then she glanced longingly over at the bed. No matter how hard and lumpy it might be, it had to be better than the floor.

"You can have half of the bed. I'll even take the side next to the wall." As if claiming the spot for his own, Noah walked over and set a small bag which she guessed held his tooth-brush and shaving gear. She had never shared a bed with a man, any bed, but this wasn't exactly *sharing* it. They simply needed to sleep. And she almost laughed at the notion of her virtue being anything *but* safe, given his unhappy looks at her.

"I'll take the other half." She pointed at the bed.

His eyebrows rose. She guessed he hadn't expected that of her. But she never in her entire life had slept in anything but a bed—and a comfortable bed at that. She hadn't toured Europe after college and slept in hostels as many that age did. She'd stayed in luxury hotels. Her mother and father had insisted.

She decided to be useful. "Should I heat something up for dinner?"

"I always have steaks the first night out. When I packed the ice chest this morning, I thought a buddy was coming, so you get your own. We'll cook them on the stove. They don't seem to have a grill, so this will have to do."

Rachel took down what she thought would be the right size of pan, a large cast-iron skillet that hung from a hook in the ceiling beside several other pans. Setting it on the stove, she asked, "We're using their things?"

"I'm going to leave them some cash to more than cover anything we've used. They will understand. We do have to hope the owner doesn't arrive between now and tomorrow morning and boot us out. Oh, and don't try to start the stove. I need to go outside and turn on the propane first."

Once he'd done that, he came inside and lit a burner. She put the pan on it, added the steaks, and hoped for the best. She'd never had time to learn to cook beyond the basics. She could boil water and scramble eggs like a champ.

The weight of everything that had happened earlier was heavy on her heart now that she had a moment to breathe. She had never been someone who lied even for a second. No white lies. Nothing but the truth. It was part of her belief system. And yet the practical joke had sounded so harmless and fun this morning when his mother proposed it.

"Noah, I'm sorry."

He stopped rooting through the ice chest and stared down at the floor. Then he looked up at her with sadness in his eyes. She felt like he was revealing a piece of himself. He said, "I'm not angry. I'm embarrassed. An 'Irish'—" he made air quotes around the word "—accent so intrigued me that I didn't try to see beyond it. That's embarrassing. And the fact that my mother knew me that well . . ." He shook his head. "That's probably even more embarrassing."

"I promise to be honest with you for the rest of this journey, however long it lasts."

He gave her a single nod. "Thank you. Now let's try to forget this ever happened." He stood, brushed his right hand off on his pants, and extended it to her. "Let's start over. I'm Noah O'Connell."

"Rachel Fitzpatrick."

He studied for a moment. "That's your real name? You actually have an Irish last name?"

Her blue eyes sparkled, and she laughed. "I do. And my father's side of the family is from a county not too far from Dublin."

"This is making more sense to me now. You told my mother your name, right?"

"Yes."

"And she proposed her idea?"

"Of course. Right after I complimented her outfit with the flowers."

He laughed so hard that he fell onto his backside and sat on the floor with one leg on either side of the ice chest.

"I don't know what she was thinking by asking me to use a fake accent. How is that alone a joke?"

"I know. She was matchmaking."

Rachel sputtered. "I was going to be in the airplane with you for, what, forty minutes? I did wonder about it, though, but I'm only here for a week. Maybe not even that."

"She's always hopeful. And she's not very good at matchmaking. Believe me, my four brothers and I have endured many attempts over the years." He paused. "Of course, maybe this time she really did just mean it as a practical joke and nothing else." He stood with some vegetables in his hands. "Let's get dinner ready, and I'll tell you about her previous matchmaking attempts while we eat."

Rachel smiled as she worked on dinner. The steaks seemed to be cooking right. Noah came over beside her and put together the salad he'd brought the ingredients for.

As they ate steak that required a fair amount of chewing, Noah swallowed a bite, then asked, "Is well-done your preference for steak?"

"Medium. I should tell you that even though I'm interested in cooking, I haven't had time to learn."

He ate another bite, chewing slowly and deliberately. After he swallowed, he said, "That's okay. But next time, I'm making dinner."

After swallowing her bite of steak and washing it down with water, she said, "That's a deal. Maybe you can show me how."

"As long as you promise not to surprise me with a homemade meal for a while."

They both laughed.

She'd enjoyed her chewy steak because of her new friend, Noah. She'd only be in Alaska for a short while, and with

Noah for even less time, but having a friend here right now would be very nice. A handsome one who made her heart beat faster made it even better.

Her mind told her to relax. Her body refused to cooperate. Sheets and blankets sealed in a plastic bag in a cupboard meant they'd been able to make the bed. Noah had thoughtfully chosen to sleep on top of the sheets, so they couldn't accidentally touch. She'd had plenty to eat with the salad, steak, and the cookies he'd brought out for dessert. She thought she'd relaxed over the meal and as they'd talked afterward.

That should have been enough to help her unwind, but she couldn't sleep. And she *knew* she needed sleep for whatever happened tomorrow. They were lost in the wilds of Alaska. Noah seemed to know his way around a wilderness, but she didn't. She tried counting sheep again.

Noah snorted as he rolled over. The man could probably sleep anywhere.

Zeke made a sound like a human sigh. Maybe he couldn't sleep either. Or maybe she was reading something more into a dog's sigh than she should.

"Zeke?" She put her hand out of the covers. A few scuffling sounds later, he bumped her hand with his nose. She scratched behind his ears. "It's okay, boy." He moved away from her, she assumed to lie down and sleep.

Ten seconds later, he leaped onto the bed between them. The mattress under her shimmied.

A crunching sound caused Noah to sit up abruptly. "What happened?"

The bed crashed to the floor, catapulting her onto the floor and sending a big dog and Noah into a pile on top of her.

"Oomph." The air whooshed out of her.

She stayed still. Even Zeke didn't move.

"Are you okay, Rachel?"

"I'm fine. Only a bit stunned to have a dog and a man fly off a bed and land on me."

Noah chucked.

She giggled, which turned into laughter.

Noah sat up, also laughing. The flashlight he'd brought out of his backpack as they'd gotten ready for bed came on. "I'm not sure we can fix this bed frame tonight. Let's pull the mattress onto the floor and see what's going on when we have more light."

The two of them and Zeke stood. Noah stepped over near the door and called his dog over. When he came to him, Noah told him to "sit and stay." The dog did as told.

The two humans dragged the mattress off the bed, filling the rest of the cabin with it. Then they worked together to make the bed. Zeke watched them carefully.

"Noah, this happened when Zeke jumped onto the bed."

He paused and glanced over at his dog. "He usually sleeps on a dog bed on the floor. I don't know why he would do that."

Rachel chewed her lip. "It might be because I talked to him and then petted him."

Noah turned to Zeke. "Did a woman corrupt you, boy?"

The flashlight provided enough light that Rachel could see the dog's tail swish across the floor in response.

"Sorry."

"Don't worry about it. Let's all go to sleep." Noah lifted his side of the covers and slid under them.

She watched Zeke, still sitting patiently by the door, as she got into bed. She'd never had a dog but had found being around this one enjoyable. "Can Zeke sleep between us?" That sounded like a good idea for more than one reason.

Noah yawned. "I hope he won't think he can do that when I get home. There isn't much room elsewhere, though, so why not?" He made a clicking sound, then called Zeke over. The mattress moved as the dog climbed onto it and stretched out.

Rachel felt her eyes close as the dog's warmth sank into her.

CHAPTER FOUR

*N*oah woke up and stretched. When his arm touched something, he turned to look and found a woman asleep beside him. Rachel. Yesterday's events came rushing back. He'd managed a perfect landing on a dry flat airfield that came out of nowhere.

And he was currently in bed with her. Sort of. His dog still lay between them.

Zeke opened one eye, closed it again, and snuggled closer to Rachel.

Even before Noah checked his watch, the half-light coming through the window told him that it must be about five in the morning. He set the covers aside gently so he wouldn't disturb Rachel and scooted down and out of bed. He'd let her sleep another hour, and then they had to get moving.

He hoped they'd either find their way to civilization today—civilization meaning a human who could help them —or that they would at least find shelter as good as this in which to spend their next night. He sat on one of the chairs and pulled his boots back on, lacing them up, grateful he had dressed for a hike. And at least Rachel had worn sneakers. Even with five sons who loved the outdoors, his mother might have shown up in high heels decorated with flowers.

He used the facilities in the outhouse behind the cabin, then went back to get his dog. He pushed the door open. "Zeke," he said as loudly as he dared. No response. "Zeke, walk." That always worked. At that, the dog's tail moved a little bit, but the allure of the warm bed was holding him there. "Zeke, come now." The tone of his voice must've been enough because Zeke stood, hopped down, and came over to his master. He did the doggie stretch of leaning forward on his legs and then back and yawned.

When they were outside, Noah patted his leg and Zeke fell into step beside him. He actually wanted him here because he would provide a super dog nose to pick up on something that his owner might miss.

He followed old vehicle tracks from the cabin for probably half a mile before he came upon another small cabin and then the road. Not a road in the traditional Western sense, at least not at this point in time. Maybe fifty years ago, but even that was up for debate. It was their way out of here, though, and their best chance of meeting another human who could help them.

He turned around and headed back to the cabin and to Rachel. He still wasn't sure what to make of her. She'd apologized for the practical joke. He'd forgiven her. His mother seemed to have combined matchmaking with a practical joke this time. In his family's tradition, he needed to find a way to show her that she needed to stop her matchmaking, and the best way to do that, at least in the O'Connell family, would be another practical joke.

Zeke trotted ahead, then turned around and came back to Noah, only to do it again. He was covering twice the miles Noah did and would be exhausted by the end of the day.

Rachel opened her eyes and saw a metal-roofed ceiling above her. When she looked to her left, she realized she was in the cabin they'd found late yesterday. Turning to her right, she expected to see Noah in bed beside her—what a strange thought that was—but he was gone. He'd taken Zeke, but left all of his belongings so he'd be back.

The evening had gone well, and they'd smoothed over their rocky start. Considering the day that they had ahead of them, as they tried to find a way back to civilization, she was glad that she had a friend rather than an enemy.

She sat up and swung her legs over the edge of the bed while rubbing her eyes. The worst thing about the evening had been discovering that the little building in the back that she'd assumed was a storage shed was actually an outhouse with a crescent moon shape cut in the door.

The silence of the empty cabin was broken by the sound of footsteps and then the door opening. She was glad to see Noah's face staring at her instead of a stranger. Or a bear.

"Rachel! Good news! I walked around the cabin to see what's nearby and found a road. Well, maybe *road* is generous. At some point in the history of this area, someone made a way for vehicles to drive here. Fortunately for us, it hasn't rained lately."

"Because?" Rachel stood and started pulling together her things and putting them back in her suitcase. Instead of having to carry her combination purse and carry-on, she dumped everything from it—including her currently useless cell phone—into her suitcase and set the purse to the side. Oh, how she wished she had brought a backpack to Alaska instead of a suitcase. But not very many people planned to be in a plane crash.

"Because it would be an impassable mudhole if it rained. Spring snow and ice melting have taken their toll on this road anyway. It's just dirt with a little gravel. But any road is the path back to civilization. People came out here to mine for gold. Most of them didn't come to live here, and they needed to be able to get back and forth with all their gear."

She eyed her suitcase. "Speaking of gear, I packed light, but I wonder if I should leave some of my clothes behind."

"Unless you have a fancy dress in there, you may need whatever you brought."

"Nothing fancy. And I did design many of these things, so I'd rather not leave them behind."

At his puzzled expression, she added, "I design clothes for fun. I even made a friend's wedding dress." She dumped everything from her large purse that acted as a carry-on into her suitcase. "I'll leave my purse behind. It's from a high-end designer, so someone may like it."

"It's more likely that they'll find it useful. I doubt most people coming this far out here would care if it was high-end." He set his ice chest to the side of the room. "To make my load lighter, I'm leaving this. I use it mostly for the first-night-out foods anyway. I *know* it will be appreciated if it's found before I can return."

As Rachel started to close her suitcase, she stared longingly at her toothbrush and toothpaste.

"I also found a stream not very far away. We can get some water there, and you can brush your teeth if you'd like."

Rachel's gaze whipped around to Noah. How had he guessed that's what she was thinking?

"You were giving your suitcase a fond look," he said in explanation. "Let's get our gear together, lock this place up, put the key back over the door in that fine hiding spot," he grinned, "and head over there."

"Is the stream's water safe to drink?"

Noah shrugged. "In my family, we always said that if it ran over rocks swiftly for a distance, then the water was clean. I don't know if that's a myth, but none of us ever got sick. I do have a water purifier with me for one person to drink. You can use that if you'd like."

There he was being sweet again. It was a good thing she wouldn't be spending any more time with this man after they got out of here. She did not want to form any attachments, since she had a life to return to in Virginia. After another quick visit to the outhouse, they left, Noah leading the way. Five minutes later, Rachel could see what he meant about the road. There were deep ruts in it from vehicles that had driven over it after rain. But it was easier than trying to push through the brush and trees on the side of the road.

They walked in silence for close to an hour, and she didn't really mind it for a while. Step after step brought them closer to somewhere, but was it the correct somewhere? She broke the silence. "Noah, are you sure this road is going in the right direction?"

"Turn around and look behind you."

Rachel did as he asked. As she turned, she saw the most magnificent sight of her life. A towering, snowcapped mountain rose from the earth to the sky. She gasped.

"Mt. McKinley, meet Rachel."

"I have never seen anything like that. At least not this close."

Noah stepped up beside her, and they both stared at the mountain for a moment before he tugged on her sleeve. "Time to go, Rachel. But know that if that mountain is behind us, we're going in the right direction."

She nodded, gave the mountain one last glance, and turned. "I will come back here to go to that park."

"Alaska's already working its magic on you, isn't it?"

"Is it? I guess it is if I'm already planning my return visit."

"And you haven't even seen it under the best of circumstances."

"That's for sure."

They both continued down the road. Sore places on her heels made her suspect that blisters were forming. When she stepped on a stone, she winced. She clearly wasn't used to this much walking in a day.

Noah said, "I only know your name and that you're from Virginia. Why are you in Alaska, Rachel?"

Conversation would take her mind off of her feet. "I came here to find my brother. He visited Alaska, met a woman, and decided to stay in Talkeetna. My parents want him to return and resume his position in the family business."

"Your parents want? What if *he* wants to stay where he is?"

"The family business comes first. It always has." Not for the first time, she wondered if that's how life *should* be.

"You work there too?"

"It's the only place I've worked since college."

"Can't you take over for him?"

She laughed. "Women don't run Fitzpatrick's." Once again, she envisioned herself in the office marked *President*, but pushed it out of her mind. The next male heir would run it, and that was final.

"Seriously? Alaska is . . . more equal. What do you do in your spare time?"

"When I have time, and that's rare, especially during the holiday season, I design women's clothing." She fingered the aqua and turquoise shirt she wore. "This is one of my designs. I unwind doing that." When he didn't say anything else, she asked, "What about you?"

"I fly."

She laughed. "I guess you have your perfect job if that's also your hobby."

As they continued in silence, the shades of green of the land and the blue sky came together in her mind into an outfit she'd sew when she got home.

CHAPTER FIVE

a roaring sound grew louder and louder. Rachel hoped the river they were approaching, one guaranteed to have quite a bit of water in it by the sound, hadn't washed out the bridge. Moments later, they rounded a bend in the road, which abruptly became water. Noah reached out to stop her from falling in. She wobbled on her feet for a moment and then stood steady.

He watched the water as it ran over the rocks. She knew they didn't have any choice but to cross it.

"Take off your shoes and socks and roll up your pant legs," he shouted over the roar of the water.

She pointed at the river. "We aren't going in there, are we?"

"It's the only sure way to civilization."

She stared at the river. In a voice she knew he could barely hear, she said, "Noah, this is a raging river. People don't walk across raging rivers and survive." She looked at him with a pleading expression in her eyes.

"Look around you. If we don't cross this river here, it

could be worse if we try to follow it further down. This is where the road goes."

"Ha! A road? This is barely a path."

"Maybe where you're from that's true. Here, if a vehicle can roll down it, it's a road. See the smooth section directly across from us? That's where the road begins again."

Noah walked alongside the river, going up and then down. About ten feet upriver, he stopped. "I think this is the best place to cross. It's wider here and shallower."

Rachel joined him. "That means it's safest here?"

"Let's hope it's the only one we need to cross." The words he didn't say concerned her.

She took off her shoes and socks as Noah had instructed. When she'd booked a reservation to come to Alaska, the trip had seemed easy. Her brother was in a town. He wasn't in the middle of the wilderness. When her parents had asked her to go get David and bring him home, she'd never pictured anything like this.

But how could you picture an adventure that you didn't know was possible?

Noah knotted the shoestrings of his boots around his neck. He tucked his socks into his pockets and rolled his pants up as high as they would go. She followed suit.

Then he surprised her by rooting around in his backpack and bringing out a length of rope. "I'm going to tie this around my waist and your waist. If one of us falls, the other may be able to ground us and keep us from being washed into the current."

"Was that supposed to be comforting?"

"It's the best I've got."

"What about Zeke?"

Noah pulled out the dog's leash. "I'll walk across the river first, carrying Zeke, and tie him to a tree. Then I'll return for you."

"But you'll have to cross the river three times."

He nodded slowly.

"Could you carry Zeke and wear your backpack at the same time?"

"Yes, but I wouldn't be able to help if your footing slipped."

Rachel eyed the river in front of her. Fitzpatricks didn't give up easily. "I can do it."

Noah looked at her as if appraising the situation. "Okay. The biggest hazard here is that the water is snowmelt and colder than you can imagine. It's also powerful. Your feet are going to get cold quickly, and that's going to make it harder for you to feel the ground. We need to move as quickly as we can and still move safely."

Every time she thought she had the situation under control, another layer of Alaska's wilderness was added on top of it. "I can do this. Don't worry, Noah." She put her shoulders back, picked up her suitcase, and walked over to the edge of the river.

Noah picked up Zeke in his arms, and they stepped into the water. At first, the water was only around her lower legs, but after a few more steps, it rose to above her knees, and the current's force against her legs tried to push her over. She steadied herself and took another step and another after that. The cold almost accomplished what the current hadn't when her legs and feet started to become numb. By the time they stepped onto the opposite shore, she wasn't sure she had feet anymore.

Standing on what Noah had dubbed a road, relief surged through her. They'd made it. "I'd do a happy dance of excitement right now if I could feel my feet enough to make sure I wasn't going to fall and break a leg."

Noah laughed. "Let's dry off and move on. We have a long day ahead of us."

Rachel sat down on a big rock beside the river and used one of the T-shirts out of her suitcase—it could be washed later—to dry off her legs before putting her socks and shoes back on and rolling her pant legs down.

As they continued down the path, Noah whistled a tune she didn't recognize as he walked with Zeke at his side. He was a few feet ahead of her, so he crested a hill before her and stopped mid-whistle. Then he let out a long, low whistle that made her hair stand up.

When she stepped beside him, she saw why. The river in front of them was even worse than the last one.

"Rachel, I don't think we can safely cross here. It won't last much longer, but we're still above treeline, so it's pretty easy to walk through the brush. Let's follow along the side of this hill and hope that we find a better place to cross."

"I don't think words could make me happier than what you just said."

They did that and reached a point where the river broadened. "We can cross here. Just do what we did last time." This time, Zeke lay down once he was on the other side and seemed to want to take a nap. She felt the same. But they continued down the road.

"Noah, I hope this is a real road. Why haven't we seen any cars or trucks yet?"

"First, most cars couldn't make it. It would only be trucks because they'd need to have high enough clearance to get through the water and not flood out. It's also the first part of May and not that long after the snow melted this year. I don't think most people will start using their cabins until about Memorial Day. That's when we Alaskans see the switch between winter and summer. It might be even later than that here."

"No spring?"

"Spring here is often called breakup. The snow and the ice melt and break up. We don't have that pretty season when all the flowers bloom and the birds sing, it's all wonderful again, and the temperatures rise. Spring is a season that I sometimes miss."

She glanced over at him with a questioning expression.

"I went to college in Oregon and then joined the Navy. I was stationed in a few places that had an actual spring."

"I didn't realize you'd ever lived outside of Alaska. What brought you back?"

He stopped and gestured with his arm, motioning to the land around them. "Right now, we're just trying to survive. But if we came prepared and knew what we were getting into, this would be a place I would love to explore. It's the nature, the raw beauty. I haven't found this anywhere else, at least not in the United States."

Clouds skittered across a blue sky. A plane flew overhead, and Noah held his hand up to shield his eyes against the sun to watch it. He probably wished he was up there flying instead of here on the ground. The day continued with them only having to ford two smaller streams. The brush changed to trees, some pine trees that Noah said were black spruce and some paper birch trees with pretty, white bark. In late afternoon, they came upon a cluster of old cabins.

As they wandered around them, Rachel said, "Are these even safe to go into?"

Noah opened one of the front doors. The inside wasn't as

dirty as she would have expected for a building that must be fifty years old or more. "I think this has been used for shelter and fairly recently." He looked around outside. "See the fire pit over there? Someone has stayed here and cooked meals there. Do we choose to stay here or keep going and hope we find something else before dark?"

Rachel felt a level of exhaustion she had never experienced in her life. Sleeping on a dusty wooden floor sounded heavenly compared to taking another ten steps. "Here."

"I was hoping you would say that. This has been a long day." Noah smiled encouragingly at her. "We covered quite a few miles." His words were encouraging, but his tone wasn't. When she stared at him, waiting for him to say more, he added, "I'm fairly certain we have many miles in front of us before we reach civilization."

"I'll focus on the miles we've covered."

"That's a good idea."

Zeke, seeming to understand that their hiking was over for the day, stretched out on the ground.

Noah instructed her on finding dry wood for the fire, so Rachel walked around doing that while he started setting up their camp. A couple of hours later, they'd eaten a wonderful meal, of what she wasn't sure, but something from his backpack that came out of pouches. They sat on large pieces of tree trunk someone had placed around the campfire.

She looked up at the sky. "My dream is that a truck somehow drives down this road and whisks us away to that wonderful lodge where I have reservations."

He laughed. "I have to tell you that you impressed me today."

She glanced up at him, startled, and pointed at her chest. "How did *I* do that?

"You crossed every stream without complaining. You may not realize this, Rachel Fitzpatrick, but you have the makings of an Alaska woman."

Rachel smiled. "I appreciate the compliment. But I'm here for a reason. My brother came to Alaska and decided to stay. He has to run the family business and I work in that business. I have a life in Virginia that we both have to return to soon."

Noah watched her, the flicker of the firelight playing off her red hair as the sun set. The buttoned-up Easterner he'd met yesterday morning had changed, but she didn't see the change yet. Maybe she never would.

Rachel made a bed for them on the floor. Noah's emergency blanket went down first. They both laid on it side-by-side, pulling his sleeping bag over them. She folded up some of her clothes and put them behind her head as a pillow.

It was the most uncomfortable bed she'd ever been on in her life. Could an exhausted person manage to sleep on this, or would she be awake all night?

The next thing she knew, Rachel opened her eyes to darkness, reached to her left for her bedside table, and only found air. Panic welled up inside her, and then she remembered where she was.

She was alone with a man who had been a stranger two days ago, sleeping on the floor of a cabin that could well collapse in the night. She'd been courageous. She'd been strong. She pulled on every resource she had inside herself. But she didn't have any more to give.

A single tear slid down the side of her cheek. She wiped it away with the palm of her hand. Then another and another fell. Zeke, seeming to sense her distress, whimpered. She heard rustling sounds, and he curled up next to her on the floor.

"It's okay, boy." She gulped and sobbed at the same time, trying to calm down. She had to hold herself together.

"Rachel? Is something wrong?" Noah asked in a sleepy voice.

Never be the weak woman. She'd learned that lesson well in a male-oriented business. *Never let them smell fear.* "No. I'm fine." She sniffed and gulped.

He sounded more awake when he said, "You aren't okay. Give me your hand." She reached toward him, and he clasped her hand snugly in his.

"We're going to get out of here. Don't worry."

She sniffed. "Are you only saying that to make me feel better?"

"I've never been very good at that sort of thing, so, no, I'm not. We're on a road. We're in an area where I know people come in the summer. There are fish in the streams. We're going to be fine."

She squeezed his hand and felt sleep coming back over her. "You're wrong about not being good at comfort. Thank you, Noah."

The next thing she knew, filtered sunlight shone through a small, multi-paned window covered with years of grime. She'd survived.

She prayed that today was the day they were rescued.

Noah stood outside their cabin while Zeke did his doggy business. What had happened last night? He'd never been a warm and fuzzy sort of guy. At least he'd never seen himself that way. But last night, Rachel had reached inside him in a way no one else ever had. And he'd found a way to make her feel better.

He had to make sure she didn't touch his heart any other way because she was leaving. She had made herself quite clear about that.

She had a full life back in Arlington. A life it wasn't easy to walk away from. Although something about her brother's situation didn't feel right. The man came to Alaska on a whim, met a woman, and decided he was going to stay here because of her. No one decided those things that quickly. People didn't fall in love that fast. Oh, he knew there was that love at first sight thing, but he didn't particularly believe in it. Maybe love over months, but not days.

He hoped and prayed that they would be rescued today, so she didn't work her way any closer to his heart.

And he definitely needed to find a way to pay his mother back for her joke.

When he and Zeke went back into the cabin, he found Rachel rolling up his sleeping bag. She'd restored everything else to the way they'd found it.

"Do you have a plan for today, Noah?"

He laughed. "Other than getting rescued?"

At that moment, he realized that she had her head down and was focused on the ground, not at him. She usually looked him in the eye, a quality he rather liked. Especially with her bright-blue eyes. He shook himself. No, he wouldn't let his thoughts go there. But something was clearly wrong. She stood and said, "I think we're ready to go," to the general direction of the wall to his left.

"Rachel, what's going on?"

Startled eyes looked up at him. She opened her mouth as if to speak, then she closed it again.

He stared at her, silently waiting.

"I'm embarrassed. I was at a low last night. I have never let anyone see me cry."

She couldn't be older than mid- to late-twenties, and she'd always had to cry alone? He'd always had brothers and parents who cared about him. "Not even your parents or your brother or some other relative? A friend?"

She shook her head. "I always had to be strong."

Before he gave it any thought, he stepped forward and pulled her into a hug. With his arms around her, he moved his upper body back a few inches and looked at her face. "You can be real around me."

Her eyes slowly dropped to his mouth. She reached up on tiptoes and leaned in to give him a kiss as light as a butterfly's touch. Before he could give it a second thought, she'd stepped back and it was over.

Rachel bit her lip. "I'm sorry, Noah. I shouldn't have done that."

He wasn't sure exactly what to do. Instead, he defused the moment by saying, "No problem. We're friends, right?" A friend who might like to kiss her again sometime.

She smiled. "Friends sounds good."

"Well, let's get going. We can't get rescued if we don't find people, right?" He added all the enthusiasm he had to those words.

Rachel picked up her suitcase. "I'm ready."

*a*n hour later, the blisters on her heels seemed to have blisters on top of them. Every step hurt. When they came over the crest of a hill on the road, there before them was one more river to ford. It was probably the same stupid river that they kept crossing over and over again. At this point, she felt like she was getting a grip on whether the crossing would be straightforward or more complicated.

She sat down on the edge of the road and started unlacing her sneakers. "I keep hoping we've crossed our last time."

"You and me both." Noah sat down beside her and began working on his boots. "I'm glad that tying us together doesn't seem necessary any longer."

When they were ready, Noah reached to pick up Zeke, but his dog backed away from him. The roar of the water must have unnerved him too. "Come on, boy. We're going to make it." Something in his tone of voice must have convinced the dog because Zeke let him pick him up, they stepped into the water, and he held his elbow to the side. She slipped her arm through it, and the three of them entered the water.

Step by step, they waded across the river's icy water. The one good thing about it was that she couldn't feel her blisters after thirty seconds. At about the middle of the stream, the river channel had more volume of water than normal. When her foot slipped on a rock, she held on to Noah's arm more tightly.

"We're almost there, Rachel. Hang on."

As he spoke those words, Noah's right foot dipped lower than it had before and caught him off balance. She held onto his arm and tugged him in her direction to keep him on his feet, but she slipped in the process.

"Let go, Rachel! Zeke and I are going to take you down."

She refused to let go and held on tight.

Noah struggled with his footing, finally finding solid ground again. As he stood upright, her angle changed abruptly and she slipped, the water catching the edge of her suitcase and dragging her lower body into the current. She found her footing and jerked the suitcase from the water as they stepped forward.

When they finally reached the other side, Rachel dropped to the ground and rested her hands in her face. "I didn't think we were going to make it."

Noah took off his backpack and dropped to the ground, and Zeke sat beside him, pressing himself against his owner for comfort.

She tugged her soggy suitcase over and opened it. Everything she saw was soaked, including her phone, which dripped water when she held it up. "I hope your backpack is drier than my suitcase."

"That's too bad about your phone. But everything in my

pack should be fine. I use waterproof bags, so it can rain while I hike and not be a disaster."

He opened up the top of it and felt around inside. "The bottom of the pack is a bit damp, but the food and everything else is okay." He checked the sleeping bag that hung underneath his pack, and discovered that it was wet. "I apparently did not buy the highest quality waterproof bag for the sleeping bag. Or perhaps waterproof and able to withstand the sheer volume of water in that river are not the same thing."

As those words sank into Rachel's head, she gasped.

"Yes. We don't have a sleeping bag to use as a blanket tonight. Only the emergency blanket. We won't freeze." He stood and, in a voice that wavered slightly, said, "Let's get moving and do our best to get rescued today."

Rachel shivered and realized that not only had the dip in the river left everything below her waist soaked, but she didn't have anything dry to put on. Her teeth chattered, and she rubbed her hands on her arms to warm up.

Noah, with his backpack on, stood in front of her. "Rachel, you need to get into something dry *now*, or you'll get hypothermia, and we'll have a medical emergency."

She shook her head. "My suitcase got wet. I have a pair of socks and a pajama top that are almost dry in the middle of my suitcase."

He studied her before saying, "You'll have to roll up the pant legs and maybe tie some rope around your waist as a belt, but I do have dry clothes." He took his pack back off and pulled out of a pair of light wool pants. "I'll turn my back. You put these on, and we'll figure out what we need to do to make them work."

She nodded. As soon as he turned around, she was on her

feet and stripping off the soggy jeans. Did anything feel worse than wet jeans against your skin? If it did, she didn't want to experience it. She pulled on his pants and zipped them. They were inches too big in the waist and the length. She leaned down and folded the bottom up so she could walk and they wouldn't drag in dirt, then fisted up the excess fabric at the waist.

"Noah, let's make a rope belt."

When he turned, he laughed. "I have to say that I've never seen a woman in my pants before. But you look good in them."

She felt herself blushing.

He wrapped rope around her waist, cut off the correct amount, and handed it to her. She fed it through the belt loops and tied it into a knot she hoped she could undo later. The warmth of the dry wool calmed her.

She dug into her suitcase for the socks, put them on, and slipped back into her formerly white sneakers. Then she changed into the dry and colorful pink pajama top decorated with sheep. For the first hour, her sneakers squished with every step and the socks became equally soaked. When they stopped for a quick lunch, she took off her shoes so they could hopefully dry a little bit when the sun peeked out between the clouds and warmed things up.

By the time they'd finished their lunch of cheese, sausage, and crackers, the sun was behind thickening clouds. Considering how she'd felt earlier, she could imagine what it would be like to be soaked to the skin from rain. She hoped today would be the day of their rescue.

Her not insignificant attraction to Noah did not help the situation. She still couldn't believe she'd kissed him this morning. Nice guy that he was, he'd brushed it off and hadn't said anything. Talk about a relationship that couldn't go anywhere. If anyone ever had a life waiting for them outside of Alaska, it was her. She had the next thirty years of her life mapped out. Work in the family business, maybe meet a nice man, and have children—that was still up for grabs—but stay in Alaska? No!

The blisters on her feet grew more and more irritated. She heard an engine sound. It must be another plane flying overhead unknowingly taunting her with the possibility of escape.

Noah stopped and held up his hand. "Do you hear that?"

Before she could answer, he grabbed her in his arms and spun her around and kissed her.

When he set her back down, she stared at him, wondering if he had gone mad, Noah pointed to the right, down the road. He grinned like a fool and shouted, "A car or truck. Don't you hear it?"

They waited in silence, and right when Rachel was about to conclude that his time in the wild had caused him to imagine something, like a mirage in the desert, she did hear it.

He grabbed her hand. "We're almost there, Rachel." He ran with her at his side, and she didn't care if her feet or any other part of her hurt. They went over a hill and down the other side and around a bend, the sound getting louder. Then they came to an intersection with another road. This road was in much better condition.

And there, coming down the road toward them, was a man driving a large off-road vehicle.

∽

Noah watched Trapper Creek, a small town near Petersville, pass by from the back of the pickup truck as they drove down the road toward the Parks Highway. They'd be in Talkeetna soon. He didn't think he had ever been this happy. The ATV's owner had driven them to his pickup truck, loaded his ATV onto the trailer rolling behind them, and was taking them to the lodge in Talkeetna. They had survived, and he was getting Rachel back to civilization. He'd see her tucked into her lodge, take care of his airplane, and get back to life on the Kenai.

A life without Rachel.

After spending the last few days with her, he'd started to enjoy being around her. That happened to people who were in the trenches together in war and in other situations where they had to band together to survive. He'd read about that before in true stories, and his grandfather had talked about times from his own life when that happened during World War II. You made friends in those challenging times that you kept forever, even if you were very different people in real life.

He glanced over at the woman beside him. This woman *was* very different from him. His life was here in Alaska. He knew that with absolute certainty after trying to live elsewhere.

Rachel took his hand in hers and smiled up at him as she squeezed it. "Noah, we made it." Her blue eyes sparkled.

Her life was in Virginia.

CHAPTER SEVEN

The pickup truck dropped them off at the door of the lodge where she had her reservation. The rustic beauty of the building far exceeded what she'd expected, but right now, she'd have thought anything with electricity was the best thing she'd ever seen.

Noah helped Rachel out of the truck, then lifted out her still wet suitcase and his backpack. They thanked their rescuer, paying for the gas to get them here with extra for his time, despite his protests. Then he drove away with a great story to tell.

Staring up at the building, she realized what this moment meant. She did not want to say goodbye to Noah yet, though. A way to extend their time together came to mind. "Noah, can I get you a room here to thank you for saving my life?" *Please say yes.* "If you hadn't been flying me to Talkeetna, you might have been somewhere where you could safely land nearer to civilization. Your precious baby wouldn't be out there on a runway all by herself."

"Rachel, I can't let you do that. Besides, if you hadn't been in the airplane with me, you wouldn't have had to be rescued."

She waved her hands in front of herself. "Let's call it even. But I really would like to get you a room here. Unless you have somewhere else to sleep tonight?"

He paused and shifted on his feet. "I would normally say that I could pitch a tent somewhere, but I have a soggy sleeping bag, so that isn't going to happen. And I'm not sure how much it's going to cost me to get my plane out of there. I could call people I know to try to find a friend of a friend of a friend who lives in Talkeetna and has a spare room." He frowned. "I'll let you buy me a room tonight, but I want to be able to pay you back in the future."

Rachel smiled. That would give her one more evening and morning with Noah. "Great! I hope they have another room available."

Noah laughed. "In the first part of May? We can probably have our pick of any room in the place."

When they stepped into the lobby with its soaring ceiling, rustic touches, and roaring fireplace, Rachel knew she'd chosen the perfect place to stay. When she went to check them in, Noah was proven correct about room availability. Not only did they have rooms, but they upgraded her to the best one in the lodge after hearing about their ordeal. Room keys in hand, they went upstairs and discovered that they had rooms across the hall from each other.

She unlocked her door. "I've been thinking about a long, hot bath for most of the drive over here, but I realized that I don't have any dry clothes to put on. I'm wearing the latest in borrowed fashion." She tugged on her rope belt. "I must have made quite a picture when I checked in!"

Noah laughed. "It just added to your story. Let me run

your laundry down to the front desk. They must have a washer and dryer here. If you take that long bath, you should have clothes waiting for you when you get out."

"Thank you!" She took a half-step forward to hug him, then stepped back. Being grateful from a distance would be best.

~

Rachel leaned back in the massive bathtub which sat at the far side of the bedroom. Wood logs crackled in the fireplace that the bed faced. This room was everything their accommodations last night had not been. Except for the fact that Noah wouldn't be nearby.

She flexed her feet as she stretched, and pain seared across their soles. Who knew that blisters could hurt like this? She rested her head against the back of the tub and felt the warm water unravel the stress of the last couple of days. About the time that she was in danger of becoming a prune, she got out and put on the soft robe provided by the lodge. After drying her hair, a knock at the door sounded. She hoped it was someone with her clothes. "Come in!"

A young woman entered the room with a stack of folded clothing Rachel recognized.

"Bless you. I am so glad you were able to do that for me."

"Is there anything else you need?"

Noah came to mind. "Have you seen the man I arrived with?"

"Yes, ma'am. He asked at the front desk about an airplane mechanic, and he's gone out in search of the person they recommended."

Rachel waited until the woman left, then she gleefully

dressed. She debated putting on makeup, but hadn't worn any for two days, so she decided to keep it natural for one more. She gave her sneakers an ugly stare before putting them back on, knowing they wouldn't be fully dry. Maybe she could find new shoes in town. While they had been comfortable in the store, they apparently were not meant for hiking long distances.

Feeling human again, she dumped everything out of her suitcase, grateful she'd bought a plastic one that could be wiped out. It may not have waterproof seals, but she wouldn't need that on the rest of this trip. Shampoo, makeup, and other toiletries were in plastic bags, so they were fine. Everything—except for her phone—could be salvaged.

Order restored to her life as much as possible, she headed to downtown Talkeetna in the lodge's shuttle to relax and consider what she'd say to David when she called him. That situation felt more real now that she was here. She loved her brother, but he was a few years older than her, and they hadn't spent much time together as adults. At this point, she didn't know him well.

After lunch in a charming restaurant called "Katie's Corner" where she indulged her sweet tooth with a wonderful piece of homemade apple pie, Rachel wandered around from store to store in the quirky small town to check out the retail offerings. When she stepped out of a small gift shop focused on the store across the street, she ran into a man walking by.

She stepped back. "I'm so sorry." Then she looked up into his face and gave a shriek of joy. "David?

The tall man with reddish-brown hair and tortoiseshell

glasses now wore jeans and a flannel shirt instead of a suit and tie.

"Rachel? What are you doing in Talkeetna?"

She stepped away from the store's entrance and searched her mind for an answer he wouldn't mind hearing.

Before she found one, he said, "*They* sent you, didn't they? Mom and Dad. You're supposed to straighten me out." He said the last sentence with finality, full well knowing the answer to the question.

Rachel sighed. "You know Mom and Dad."

"I do. I have hoped all of my life that they would see me as a person and not just the male heir. The next ruler of the great Fitzpatrick men's clothing dynasty."

Rachel stared at him with her jaw hanging open. He'd always been the dutiful child, the one who had embraced their parents' vision for his life and stepped in to do what was asked of him. Had it at all been an illusion?

He ran his hand over his face. "There's something I need to get home to right now. Can you come to dinner at my house?"

Something had changed about David in the three months he'd been gone. He seemed stronger. Happier. Not only happy actually, but content and at peace. "I would love to come to dinner." She didn't want to leave Noah alone, though. Or maybe she didn't want to be without him at her side, but she tucked that away to consider later. "I made a friend on the way here. Could I bring him too?"

David raised his eyebrows. "Of course. Anyone is welcome at our house. I'll text you the address."

"My phone was damaged. Just tell me what it is." She listened carefully and memorized the address.

As he turned to leave, she put her hand on his shoulder. "The friend has a dog. Zeke."

He smiled. "Bring him too." With that, he hurried away.

Her parents had sent her to Alaska for a very specific mission, to "talk some sense" into her brother and bring him home. But now that she'd seen him, she had a feeling that he had found a home here in Alaska and had no interest in a life in Virginia. She'd talk to him about it more tonight.

Back at the lodge, Rachel stowed her purchases, which included a necklace for her mother and a cribbage board for her father with a moose carved on it.

She'd love to dress up for an evening out with Noah, but not only did her wardrobe not include anything beyond casual, she also didn't think there was a whole lot of dressing up in Talkeetna. She turned a chair to face the door and left the door open so she could catch Noah when he went into his. Flipping through the local information packet that had been left in the room, she learned a lot about Talkeetna and Alaska.

Noah peered in her door around 3 p.m. "Are you so used to wide-open spaces that you don't want closed doors?"

"I wanted to see you when you got back. My brother invited me for dinner, and I asked if I could bring you." As soon as she said the words, she felt like she'd presumed too much. Now that they had been rescued, would he want to go anywhere with her, much less spend time with any member of her family?

As she was about to retract the words—or at least buffer them, so he didn't feel any obligation—he said, "I'd love to. Let me get cleaned up from working on the airplane, and I'll be over. Can I bring Zeke?"

"I asked him about that too." She smiled. "My brother said to bring him."

~

The lodge shuttle dropped the three of them off at her brother's house, but the driver would be off-duty later, and they'd need to find their own way back to the lodge after dinner. She hoped David would drive them, that they wouldn't end up at odds by the end of the evening and have to find their own way to the lodge. His home was a small log cabin, but, unlike their wilderness accommodations, it was very tidy outside. A walkway led to the front door which was painted a bright blue.

At the door, she said, "You can still back out, you know. You don't have to meet my brother."

He shrugged. "I don't see any reason why I would *not* want to meet him."

"I hope we don't make you regret coming."

When she reached up to knock, he grabbed her hand before she could touch the door. "Rachel, what's the undercurrent here? What am I stepping into? Am I going to be in the middle of something you'd rather keep in the family?"

She lowered her arm and thought about the answer to that question. Would he be? "I'll tell you honestly that I don't know. I don't know why he's chosen to live here instead of Virginia. I don't know if he's planning to stay here forever. Or if this is simply his way of temporarily escaping the life that he had there."

She raised her hand to knock and looked at Noah with one eyebrow raised.

He motioned for her to go ahead.

David answered the door immediately, grinned, and pulled her in for a hug. "I'm so happy you're here. But don't think you're going to get me back to that old job."

As she stepped through the door, she said, "Mom and Dad want to know what's holding you here. You had a life back in Arlington that you've left behind. Roots."

She was about to say that those were her parents' words, not hers, when a tall, dark-haired woman stepped out of an adjoining room, drying her hands on a kitchen towel. The woman smiled first at Rachel and Noah and then up at David with an expression that could only be called love.

That's why he'd stayed. She knew he had met someone, but this felt more permanent than she'd imagined.

Her brother leaned in and kissed the woman briefly before stepping back and saying, "Rachel, I am honored to introduce you to my *wife*, Katie."

The last few days had been a strain, enough that Rachel wasn't certain if she'd heard correctly or if she was still so exhausted that she couldn't tell reality from daydreams.

Fortunately, Noah had no such issues. He stepped forward and extended his hand to shake David's. "I'm Noah O'Connell, and I'm pleased to meet you and your wife." He reached over, put his arm around Rachel, and pulled her forward, an action that caused her brother to raise his eyebrows.

Noah's touch broke Rachel out of her stupor, and she beamed at the woman. "Katie, I am so happy to meet you."

The exuberance in her voice must have reassured everyone because David and Katie both laughed. David gave his new wife a loving glance.

"I'm very happy for you," Rachel repeated and then

blinked. "Just give me a second to process the fact that my brother is married."

Her brother eyed the arm that Noah still had around Rachel. She flushed and stepped to the left, away from Noah and his touch, something she did not want to become used to.

"I rented a car and drove from town to town, only staying a night or two in each. I had planned to be in Talkeetna overnight and then head up to Denali. But I met Katie about an hour after I arrived. We got married a month to the day later."

Rachel shook her head. "Aw, David. I wish I could have been at your wedding."

He hugged her again. "I wish you could have too, sis. But if Mom and Dad had found out, they'd have done everything in their power to stop me, including trying to bribe her."

Katie put her hand in his. With a smile on her face, she said, "I might have had to consider the amount and even ask for them to up it, just to see what you were worth. But I wouldn't have taken it."

David laughed. "Do you see why I love her?"

Actually, Rachel could.

CHAPTER EIGHT

"Please, sit down in the living room while I finish making dinner. I hope everyone likes roast chicken, mashed potatoes, and salad?" Katie said.

Zeke, who had quietly stayed near Noah thus far, gave a single bark.

Laughing, Katie bent down in front of him. "Are you hungry too?"

Zeke sniffed her shirt.

"He's greedy. He's been fed."

"The dinner you've made sounds heavenly after some of the freeze-dried food we ate." Rachel started to walk into the living room, but her brother grabbed her arm.

"What are you talking about? You've never eaten anything remotely freeze-dried."

"It's a long story." She gestured with her head toward his living room. "Let's go sit down, and I'll tell you about it."

Katie said, "Oh, no, you don't. This is something I don't want to miss. Can we talk about it over dinner?"

Rachel laughed. There was something inherently likable about this woman. Her brother's new wife. Her sister-in-law. That would take some getting used to.

David kissed his wife's cheek. "Of course we'll wait. We'll talk about some boring family stuff and torture Noah while you finish dinner."

"Oh, well, that's okay." Katie grinned and went back into the kitchen.

Rachel and Noah followed David into his comfortable living room and sat down. With its cozy sofas, a woodstove in the corner that heated the room, and the log walls, it exuded Alaskan coziness.

She wasn't sure how to begin the conversation. "Mom and Dad—"

David interrupted. "I'm not going to devote my life to Fitzpatrick's Menswear and Suits." He leaned forward earnestly. "I don't want that life."

"Maybe Katie would enjoy living in Arlington?" she suggested. She hoped her brother would answer in a way that let her do what she had been asked to do. Bring him home.

Her parents would *not* be pleased if she returned without him.

"Rachel, that's the life *you* want. It never was the life *I* wanted." David held up his hand before she could interrupt. "Maybe when I was young, right out of college, I was eager to run the chain. But year after year, I became more and more certain that I needed to escape."

Oh, she knew how he felt. But she'd invested so much of her life energy into this business that she didn't know what else she would do. And she had never purposefully let her parents down. "How will you make a living? How will you pay rent, eat, and have transportation?"

"I've been saving every penny I could for years. As CEO, they paid me well. But I lived inexpensively."

She had always wondered why he lived in a studio apartment when he could have afforded an entire house.

"This," he gestured to the house around them, "was bought with cash. The same goes for my truck. I always enjoyed woodworking but never had much of an opportunity to do it with all of the hours I worked. Every once in a while, I'd sneak away to a friend's garage, and we'd build something. I got to be pretty good at it, and now I have a shop in this backyard with electricity and heat, and I've been building and selling things. That will be my food money."

The earnest expression and sincerity on his face shocked Rachel. The brother she thought she knew hadn't been the real man, just a veneer.

David's words swirled around her, her emotions running wild. He didn't want to be in the business. She did. But she'd been born a girl. Only men were president of Fitzpatrick's. She looked David in the eye and said, "Do you think they'll let—"

"Maybe they'll let—" he said at the same time.

Noah jumped in. "I don't understand. David doesn't want to run the family business. Do you, Rachel?"

She nodded. "I've always wanted to run it. While I worked there, I got an MBA through night classes so I could try to convince my parents I was capable of it."

"Well, then this is your chance. You aren't pushing your brother out. He doesn't want the job." Noah said the words in a matter-of-fact way.

Rachel sat straight and imitated the expression her father

had when he spoke. "Fitzpatrick's Menswear and Suits is passed down from son to son. No man wants a woman helping him choose his clothing."

Noah shook his head like he couldn't figure out what she'd said. "Women work in men's clothing stores. I know because they've waited on me."

David spoke before she had a chance. "Not in the Fitzpatrick tradition. I did hire women for stores, but Dad rarely visits them anymore, so he doesn't know that. The business went from my grandfather to my father, and it was supposed to fall to me. Our parents are at retirement age, and I could see this day coming, that any second they would say it was time for me to take over. And the pressure of that made me run as far away as I could."

"They are nearing retirement. I don't remember you traveling to Alaska before this. Did you plan to move to Talkeetna all along?"

Katie stepped out of the kitchen with a platter of chicken in her hands and set it on the table. Her brother watched his wife, love clearly shining in his eyes.

"I came to Alaska because it was my boyhood fantasy." David shrugged. "It's rugged, and there are still places that are very remote. I needed to get as far away from the hustle and bustle of my daily life as I could. Two weeks into my trip, I stopped in Talkeetna. It was lunchtime, so I asked the first person I saw where the best restaurant was. She pointed me to Katie's Corner." Katie came out of the kitchen with two more serving bowls and set them down.

"I had lunch there! The apple pie was fabulous."

Katie smiled at her. "I'm glad you enjoyed it because we're having it for dessert tonight."

Rachel glanced at Noah. "You're going to love dessert."

David continued as his wife went back to the kitchen, immediately returning with another bowl, which she set on the table. "She's a great cook. I went in Katie's Corner, sat down, and ordered," David continued. "One of her waitresses had sprained her ankle earlier that morning, so Katie herself took my order. I asked her out, and we got married soon after that." He stood and the rest of them followed suit.

Noah turned to his dog and said, "Zeke, you stay here." The dog obeyed, seeming happy to lie by a warm wood stove.

As Rachel walked up to the table, her mouth watered. The mashed potatoes had flecks of what must be herbs in it, and the salad wasn't a simple green salad. It had a lot of additions, including strawberries and nuts, her favorite kind of salad. "So you married the owner of the restaurant? That's so sweet."

Noah took his seat at the table. "It's actually very smart." He put a large portion of chicken on his plate and passed the platter to Rachel. "It is true that a man's heart can be reached through his stomach."

Katie laughed. "I've heard that line so many times since we got married."

Rachel ate her food and participated in the conversation every once in a while. David's news was nothing short of a bombshell. He was supposedly on a brief hiatus, as his parents had called it, sowing his wild oats. Now he had a wife, a home, and a new business, all part of a new life.

After Katie served the apple pie and sat again, David took her hand. "We have news to share. Being able to share it with you in person, Rachel, is so nice. I've always loved you. Know that."

Rachel's eyes started filling with tears, and she had to

blink them back. They weren't a family that ever expressed emotion. At least not positive emotion.

Turning back to his wife, he said, "Not long after Christmas, we're going to welcome our first child."

The tears she'd held back started rolling down her cheeks. Laughing and crying, she stood and leaned over to hug her brother and then his wife. "I'm so excited for you." After a pause, she said, "And I get to be an aunt!"

David laughed. "Yes, you do."

After dessert and more conversation about their recent adventures, Rachel and Noah put on their jackets by the front door. Her brother did the same, then pulled out his car keys.

"Having you here, Rachel, has been a huge blessing. You too, Noah. Sis, I don't envy you telling the folks. But I am going to leave it to you. There's no point in them trying to bully me back to Virginia, and I know that's what would happen."

Rachel was silent on the short drive back to the lodge. David must have felt the same as she did about the business. She wanted to work there but struggled with her parents regularly. When they pulled up to the lodge, her brother said, "Will I have a chance to see you again before you leave?"

She turned toward him, barely able to see his face in the light from the front of the lodge. "I'm not sure when I'm leaving, but I will be back. You can be sure of that, David. My nephew or niece is definitely going to know his or her aunt. You keep me updated all the way, okay?" She gave him a firm stare.

"Yes, ma'am. There is a little bit of Dad in you, you know."

Rachel rolled her eyes. "Don't be mean like that."

David laughed.

She and Noah stepped out, and Zeke jumped to the ground. They stood in the cool night air as her brother drove off.

Noah put his hand on her arm. "That was a big deal, wasn't it?"

They turned to go inside. "Yes. I'm happy for him, though. You know, Noah, it's going to make big changes in the family business." Excitement flashed through her. "If—and that's a big if—they let me take over, I will finally get the job I've been trying to get for years. Noah, you might be talking to the next president of Fitzpatrick's Menswear and Suits." They entered the lodge.

"When do you find out?"

"I'll call my parents early tomorrow morning. It's best to talk to them between eight and nine, before the stores have opened and they've had to deal with anything stressful." She laughed again and turned and hugged Noah.

When he froze and stared at her face, she wondered if he would kiss her. Then the lights around them caught her eye, and she realized where they were. In the middle of the lodge's lobby. No one was watching them, but it was far from private.

Pulling back and changing the subject, she asked, "Are you going to be able to get your plane going tomorrow?"

"That's the plan. I've been fortunate to find what I believe it needs to get it started again. A mechanic and I will fly out there again in the morning in a helicopter. I think I'm going to be able to fly it off the runway."

"Where to then? Are you going to finish your vacation?"

He chuckled. "I think I've had all the rugged outdoors that I want for a little while. I'll save those days off for later."

"So you're flying home to Kenai?"

"No. I'm going to drop my plane off in Anchorage and have it thoroughly checked out from top to bottom."

Rachel extended her hand. "Then this may be goodbye. I may never see you again." That thought caused her so much pain. Even though she hadn't known the man a few days ago, he'd become an important part of her life.

He quirked an eyebrow. "I think we're beyond that, aren't we, Rachel?" He didn't move any closer. He just watched her.

She gave a nod. Then he leaned forward and without touching her anywhere else, gave her a sweet kiss. A goodbye kiss. When it ended, she silently turned away, walked into her room, and closed the door. She felt like a little piece of her had been left behind with Noah, but it wasn't possible to feel like that about someone she'd only met a few days earlier.

She saw her sad face in the mirror near the door. "Cheer up, Rachel," She told herself. "In the morning, you will be on your way to becoming the new president of the company." That put a grin on her face.

Rachel woke to the buzzing of the alarm on the clock in her room, which she had set to 4:00 a.m. When she'd showered and dressed, she twisted her hair into an updo and put on makeup. Looking the part might give her a layer of armor against what might happen. She made the call at 8:30 a.m. Eastern time.

As usual, her mother answered her father's phone. Rachel didn't waste any time. "Mother, I found David."

"Harold, come over here. It's Rachel." She heard scuffling as the phone was put on speaker.

"What did he have to say for himself?" Before she could come up with an answer for that vague question, he continued, "Where is he, and when is he coming home?"

"He's living in Talkeetna, as we thought."

She heard the tapping of computer keys and then her mother's voice. "That's a very small town. Is it as much in the middle of nowhere as it appears on this map?"

"It's a couple of hours from the biggest city, Anchorage, but there are some other things around." Including a handsome pilot across the hall, but that was more information than her mother needed.

After more tapping, her father said, "Seats are available for you and David to fly back to Arlington tomorrow." Her father had a way of stating what should be a question.

This is when it would either get really ugly or maybe, just maybe turn out well for her. Or both. "David doesn't plan to come back to Arlington."

Her mother spoke. "I don't understand, Rachel. How can he run the company from Talkeetna, Alaska?" Her mother said the word Talkeetna very slowly and deliberately as though it was a very foreign word.

"That's the point, Mother. He isn't planning to return."

Her father's voice became more gruff. "That won't work. You need to do your job, and get your brother back here."

He also had a way of making her feel like she was five years old again. "Father, he isn't coming back." She said every word deliberately so that he could understand. "He's married."

Silence greeted her, then her mother spoke. "I don't

understand. Rachel, did you say that David is married? We had someone nice for him to meet when he came back."

Oh, he would have loved that. *Not.*

"If he's married, he can bring her along." He still didn't understand. But since he was an intelligent man, it was more likely that he didn't want to understand.

She tried not to sigh out loud. "David is married, and the woman he's married to owns a restaurant in Talkeetna. They aren't going anywhere."

When silence greeted her again, she added, "As for the position of president, I've told you for years that I was capable of doing that."

Her father laughed. "Women don't run Fitzpatrick's."

"Father, while David's been gone, I have done the majority of the work running Fitzpatrick's. I can be the CEO." Her heart raced in excitement because he had to agree. There was no other option unless he was going to hire a stranger, and she didn't see him ever doing that.

Her father spoke again, but in an amused tone of voice she wasn't used to hearing. "Your mother and I discussed this possibility, and we came to a conclusion about what we would do if David didn't come back. We put some feelers out to see if there would be interest."

"Interest in what? Someone else to run the company?"

"No, dear," her mother replied. "To buy the company."

Rachel sat down. "Sell Fitzpatrick's?" Her head swam at the news. Everything she had worked for all of her life would be gone? As a child, she'd helped in the stockroom. Every class she'd taken in college had been focused on her future at Fitzpatrick's. She'd gone to Chamber of Commerce meetings and more. *Everything* had been focused on Fitzpatrick's.

"Your mother and I are ready to retire. If David isn't

coming back, we can sell. I found someone who is very inter-ested. I'll let them know that we can move ahead with it. I'm sorry it had to turn out this way."

The call ended, and she stared at the phone, she didn't know for how long.

Not only would she not be president of the family busi-ness, life as she had always known it had just ceased to exist.

CHAPTER NINE

*S*he could stay and spend more time with her brother, but she wanted to come back and be around when their baby was born, so they'd spend some quality time together then. Besides, she had an obligation to return to her job and she'd do what she needed to there as long as it lasted.

Before she could go home, she needed a ride back to Anchorage. She hadn't checked, and she could be wrong, but she doubted that there were any car rental places in Talkeetna. So where did that leave her? Maybe David could drive her to Anchorage. It had been shortsighted of her not to have thought of that when they'd talked last night.

Another idea came to mind. She could fly back to Anchorage with Noah.

Should she ask him? Should she even consider spending more time with him? It was a faulty idea on many levels because she'd promised herself that she'd never set foot in another small aircraft, but she did trust Noah's skills as a pilot. Maybe not the plane itself, but definitely him. And either way, it still remained her best option.

She propped her door open again to wait for Noah and Zeke to return and considered her now very different future. What would she do after the business sold? She heard Zeke's gentle woof and footsteps on the stairs leading to the second story. She'd miss the two of them. She refused to think about how much she'd especially miss Noah. She looked out into the hall as Noah took the last step on the stairs while doing something on his phone.

"Noah?"

He glanced up from his phone.

"Will there be room on the helicopter for one more?"

Something like happiness lit his face for a moment, and then it was gone. "Are you saying you would like to come with me? To Anchorage?"

She nodded quickly before she lost her nerve.

"I know there's room on the helicopter. And the plane *will* fly today." He said those words defiantly and that unnerved her a bit. He wanted the plane to fly. That much was sure.

As long as it did, she'd get to Anchorage. And more importantly, she decided, was that she'd get to spend another day with Noah.

Rachel would be coming with him! Noah ignored the little voice that said he would have to say goodbye to her today. "You need to pack." He really noticed her for the first time today and realized that she had done her hair in a fancier way and had added makeup. She looked like she had prepared to go to work. "Be ready in about half an hour. Okay?"

"No problem. I seem to be traveling rather light." She smiled.

In his room, Noah folded everything and put it back into his backpack. "Zeke." The dog's ears perked up when he heard his name. "Rachel's going with us, so we get to spend another day with her." Zeke wagged his tail, but Noah wasn't sure if it was because he liked hearing his master's voice or because he actually understood that having Rachel with them for another day was a happy surprise.

When he opened his door, she was standing in the doorway to her room. "Grab your bag, Rachel, and let's go."

"It's already downstairs. I checked us out and was waiting for you."

He grinned. This was the first time in his life that a woman had ever waited for him. In his family, the one woman kept the men waiting.

Rachel stared at the helicopter sitting on a grassy field. A few days ago she'd never been in a small airplane. She'd also never been in a helicopter. As they approached it, she said, "I hope the helicopter stays airborne."

Noah winced. "Ooh. What a way to hurt a pilot's masculinity."

She chuckled. "Sorry. I didn't realize I said that out loud. We landed safely."

When they were seated in the helicopter, Rachel strapped in, took a deep breath, and decided to enjoy the ride.

The helicopter rose straight up, so at least there wasn't

the runway takeoff and landing. It only took a couple of minutes for them to go from being above the town to flying low but swiftly over the wilderness. Alaska from the air was nothing short of spectacular. The top of Denali stuck out from the clouds, but she knew what the great mountain looked like on a clear, sunny day.

It seemed like only a few minutes more before Noah's plane sat ahead of them on the runway. Had it only been three days ago that she'd met him? The helicopter pilot chose a reasonably flat and brush-free area near the plane, and they landed.

As they stepped out of the helicopter, she noticed impressions in mud. "What's that, Noah?"

He looked where she pointed, and his eyes got big.

CHAPTER TEN

*H*e debated the wisdom of sharing the news with Rachel that a bear had passed by that spot—and probably not too long ago, from the freshness of the tracks. Before he could decide whether or not he could tell her the whole truth, Charlie, their helicopter pilot, saw them talking and walked over. After a glance, he turned toward Rachel and said in a very matter-of-fact tone, "Ma'am, those are bear prints. And some mighty large prints too. Be grateful that you aren't spending the night out here."

Rachel made a choking sound. Noah wanted to pull her in for a hug and hold her tightly but decided that would be inappropriate with Charlie there. Or maybe it was inappropriate period now that they weren't in an emergency situation.

"Rachel, nature lives beside us, among us, and with us here in Alaska. I often hear people from other places talking about being afraid of the bears, but I have rarely seen one. We coexist."

She watched him while he said the words, then her gaze

went back to the prints. She walked away while he and Charlie started working, but Noah noticed that she stayed very close to the helicopter and her way of escape. Not that she could fly it. But he had a feeling she'd give it her best shot if it was between that and a bear. And knowing Rachel, she might figure it out.

When he could tell that the repair was going smoothly, he reached into the plane and pulled out a tool chest, a few pieces of wood, and other parts—he hoped everything he'd need to repair the bed in the cabin. "Rachel, I'm going to run over to the cabin to fix the damage." He held up the wood. "Do you want to come or stay here?"

She glanced toward the bear prints, then back at him. "There's safety in numbers. I'll go with you and watch the area while you do the repair."

Noah fought a chuckle. What would she do if she saw a bear? He helped Zeke into the back seat of the plane. "Stay here, boy. I'll be right back." He left at a fast walk, wanting to do what he needed and get back before Charlie finished. At the cabin, he talked Rachel into helping him inside.

"Are you going to use a corner brace to make it stable?" At his surprised glance, she added, "You'd be surprised at what you need to do in business. I've put things back together many times, at least well enough to wait for the company's team to get to a first-rate repair." She knelt and handed him the correct screwdriver without asking.

Surprise after surprise. He sat on the bed when he'd finished the repair. "Good as new."

"Maybe better. I think a Belgian Shepherd can jump on the bed now." She grinned.

As they walked back to the plane, Noah carrying his ice

chest and her with the purse she'd left behind, he asked, "What will you do when I get you back to the city?"

"I'm taking life one minute at a time."

That vague response made him wonder what had happened with her parents.

Charlie was finishing up when they arrived. He wiped his hands on a rag. "Turn her over. Let's see if she runs."

Noah climbed into the cockpit, turned the key in the ignition, and the plane sputtered to life. The spinning prop thrilled him beyond words.

Rachel hurried over to the plane and opened the passenger door. "Are we ready to go?" She seemed to have faith in his abilities as a pilot. That warmed his heart.

"I just need our bags."

She brushed his comment away. "I can get them." She carried his backpack and her suitcase, wedging them into the plane where they'd been before, and hopped into the airplane. What had happened to the city girl who was afraid of everything?

As they prepared for takeoff, it felt comfortable to have Rachel at his side. In a very few days, she had become a friend, only different somehow. Of course, they *had* shared a couple of kisses. But those had been in moments very different from everyday life. He wasn't sure that either of them had an idea of who they were on a day-to-day basis. He needed to learn more about her. And maybe more about himself.

Charlie moved away from the airplane and stood next to his helicopter. Noah put the plane in motion, then turned it in a half-circle to point it at the full length of runway. The engine continued running smoothly, so his stress level dropped. But they were on the ground, and the ground made it an easy fix when something went wrong.

Rolling forward faster and faster down the runway, he said a short prayer as they got to the point that the plane should lift off . . . and it did. They climbed into the air and leveled off at about three thousand feet for the flight back to Anchorage.

"It flew!" Rachel exclaimed.

He chuckled. "That makes me happy too. The engine is running smoothly, and everything seems fine. It won't be long before we're landing in Anchorage." He let out a silent sigh of relief. About ten minutes into the flight, he relaxed another notch. "Rachel, I'm sorry my mother got you into the middle of this. You might have found another way to get to Talkeetna."

A long silence greeted his comment. When he was about to say something else to bridge the gap, she spoke. "You may find this hard to believe—I find it a little bit shocking myself —but I'm not sorry. This trip forced me out of the pattern that I'd been in for a long time, years. I assumed things were one way. This trip and everything that's happened has shown me that they weren't that way at all."

Instead of being happy, she seemed sad.

"Did your parents get upset with you about David not wanting to return?"

She clenched and unclenched her hands. "Of course. He knew what he was doing when he ran. David didn't run away from something. He ran *toward* something so much better."

"He and Katie do seem like a good fit, don't they?"

She smiled. "They do indeed. I'm very happy for my brother." In the flash of a moment, her happiness turned to sadness again.

"Then what happened. What's wrong?"

She turned away as he glanced at her, but not before he saw the tears filling her eyes. "Do you remember last night when we talked about my being able to take over the business because David had left?"

He shrugged. "Of course. You said you were going to speak to your parents this morning. Did everything work out okay?"

"Oh, it's all worked out. Men run Fitzpatrick's Menswear and Suits."

There wasn't anything masculine about the woman sitting next to him. "I hope this won't sound like a sexist comment, but you're very female." He avoided the word *feminine* in case that crossed some sort of line.

"Thank you, Noah, that's sweet. But you aren't catching what I said."

He thought over her words. "Men run . . ." He paused. "You're kidding, right? They're searching for a different man to run the business, aren't they?"

"No, they aren't."

"Well, then—"

"They're selling the business. They would rather do that, Noah, than let their daughter run it. I have a degree in fashion design. When it didn't seem to be enough for them, I studied nights and got an MBA from Georgetown. *Not enough.*"

He processed what she'd said. "Very Victorian. And surprising. Not what I'm used to here in Alaska."

"Noah, it isn't what anybody has been used to for a long time. Even most conservative places would expect that a woman could rise to the top. At least that's what I would like to believe. But my parents strongly believe in tradition, and tradition says the business passes to a son. Which I am not."

They flew in silence for a while.

"Let's talk about something else," Rachel said at last. "What are you planning to do after you drop the plane off? Visit the brother you said lived near Anchorage? You can tell him about our adventure."

"I'm not ready to explain our adventure to my family."

"But it wasn't your fault, right?" She had an uncertain sound to her voice.

"Gee, thanks for the faith in the pilot, Rachel."

"Sorry. I don't know anything about airplanes. It didn't seem like you had done anything wrong. Let me say that."

He could now see Anchorage in the distance. "I didn't do anything wrong. I had the plane inspected not long ago, and nothing was found. I did a thorough preflight inspection, as I always do. It's still kind of embarrassing, though, when your plane goes down. I'm still grateful that nobody was hurt. Not even her." He patted the instrument panel. "But in answer to your question, I think it's going to be easiest if I rent a car in Anchorage and drive home. I could take a commercial flight back with the company I fly for, but I have a lot of gear and a dog." A woof sounded from the backseat.

Rachel reached over and pulled out the zipper bag with the dog treats and held it up with a questioning expression.

"He hasn't had a treat since the plane incident. Go ahead."

Rachel held the treat over her head. Crunching ensued. She smiled. "I may need to get a dog or cat when I move to wherever I'm moving to."

He turned to her quickly. "You're moving?"

"The family business is selling, Noah. I no longer have a

job. I'll go back and help them close it up. But then I have to start over."

"Are you sure that the new company won't want to keep you on?"

"I suppose that's a possibility. I hadn't considered that, but I don't know if I really want to. I might like a fresh start." She pointed into the distance. "Is that Anchorage?"

"It is." He nodded. "We're almost back. Then I need to sit down with my brothers and figure out some sort of way to play a joke on Mom after the one she played on me with your Irish accent."

Speaking with an Irish brogue, she said, "Do you mean this one?"

He laughed. "That's the one."

"What would be a joke you could play on her that would be harmless—because I wouldn't want her to be hurt in any way physically or emotionally—and very funny in the end when it was revealed?"

"I keep asking myself that very question." He adjusted a control.

"Well, let's look at it this way, what would be the worst thing that would happen to your mom—barring illness or something like that? What would she not want to happen in her world?"

Noah hesitated for a second, and Rachel noticed. "What is it? You have an idea, don't you?"

He did have one idea. He pushed it away before it could grow into something bigger, but it kept nudging at him. He radioed the tower to set up a landing at Merrill Field. Before he had to focus completely on the landing, the idea came back. "Rachel, a crazy idea keeps nudging at me. Are you in a hurry to get back home?"

"My parents weren't a hundred percent sure of what I'd find in Alaska, so I have an open-ended ticket for my return." She added in a sad voice, "It's my duty to help them with the sale, but I'm not needed as their daughter."

Without even considering it, Noah reached over, grabbed her hand, and gave it a squeeze. "Don't let those thoughts live in your head. You're needed. In fact," he was about to do something he might regret for a very long time, "I have an idea. One that Mom won't forget." There was no going back now. "I'll explain it to you when we're on the ground."

Rachel swatted at his arm. "You can't do that!"

He pointed to the swiftly approaching runway. "We've made it this far safely. I'm going to land this bird so I can get out and kiss the side of her. Then we'll find someplace where we can talk."

"Am I going to like this idea?"

"I think it will be fun."

"Then get this plane on the ground. Safely. I could use some fun."

CHAPTER ELEVEN

They landed and taxied over to a parking spot, or tie-down, as Noah called it. After they got out, he tied a rope from rings on the ground to the wings and put the triangle things in front of and behind the wheels again. "I'm going to call a taxi to have them take us over to a rental car place. One problem with having Zeke with me—"

Zeke woofed when he heard his name, and Noah reached down to scratch behind his ears.

"I am happy that you're here, boy." Zeke swished his tail in appreciation.

"As I was saying, I'd like to sit and visit with you in a coffee shop, but I don't know any that I can take a dog into. And it's not warm enough to sit outside."

"Why don't you tell me now?"

She needed to go to a store to buy a new phone, then find a room for the night and get settled into it here in Anchorage while she figured out what to do next. She had to eventually go home because she had a condo filled with her things and a family business to wrap up. Her parents didn't seem to realize how much effort she put into it. But she knew it wouldn't go nearly as smoothly if she wasn't there. No matter what, they were her parents, and she wanted to do that much for them.

"If one of my brothers eloped, my mother would be very disappointed. She has been planning our weddings since close to the day we were born. I know she loves all five of her boys, but she always wanted a daughter and really loved being able to have input when Adam married Holly. She was there every step of the way along with the mother of the bride."

Rachel watched Noah speak. What could he be thinking of that involved her?

"I realized that Mom not being there for a wedding would be distressing. It wouldn't hurt her in any way long-term when she found out it was a joke. As far as I know, none of my three remaining brothers are seeing anyone or even have a close female friend that they can do this with. That means it's up to us." He stopped talking, but he hadn't really told her what he meant.

"Up to us . . .?" Did he want her to pretend to be married to him?

He seemed frustrated that he had to spell it out. But he needed to. If he was thinking what she thought he was thinking, wow.

"If you and I pretend to be married, Mom won't be able to say anything about it, because she's the one who pushed us together."

The idea swirled around her. It was a crazy idea, but his family had a dynamic she didn't understand. They laughed together. It might be fun to hang out with them for a little while and start healing. "We only met a few days ago."

He put his hands next to his cheek in a very overacted way and sighed deeply. "Haven't you heard of love at first sight?"

She laughed.

"Will you fake marry me, Rachel?"

It was hard not to laugh again.

"I think that the proper thing to do is to get down on one knee, don't you, Noah?" She leaned back and crossed her arms.

He rolled his eyes, then dropped to one knee and grabbed her hand. "Please, Rachel, be my fake wife?"

"It's hard to turn down a proposal like that. Yes, Noah, I will be your fake wife. Until reveal and lots of laughter do us part." Smiling, she reached out her hand to help him up.

He grinned.

"Our first stop with the car has to be a phone store. It's strange not having one."

The cab pulled up, and the driver gave Zeke a not pleased look.

Noah went over to the window, and the driver rolled it down. "He's very neat, and I'll tip you extra."

The driver shrugged, and they were on their way: the future temporary Mrs. Noah O'Connell, spouse, and their furry child.

Rachel leaned against the back of the seat in the cab. What had she done? Her life had focused one hundred percent on work until she'd been sent to Alaska. Something about this O'Connell family got her to do really stupid things.

She glanced over at Noah. His furrowed brow told her he

might be trying to work out the situation as well. Maybe they could decide that it was a stupid plan and walk away. "Noah—"

"I know, Rachel, this is a stupid idea."

She saw no need to contradict the man when he was right.

"But we have to do something about my mother! She's decided that it's her mission to be the matchmaker for all of her sons and let me tell you it is not always fun when she gets rolling. The stories I could tell you." He sighed and looked out the window.

"A couple of months ago, Mom met a woman who said she flew a plane. She told this woman I'd like to meet her and sent her over to my plane where I was doing some work inside it—much like she did with you. She arrived on a motorcycle wearing leather from head to toe. Not my type. I like leather in general, but not when it's practically painted on. And the spiked hair didn't help."

Rachel grinned. "If that's the worst she can do . . ."

"No. It isn't. My poor brother Jack . . ." He shook his head sadly. "He's a photographer, so she sent him a beautiful woman to be his model. At least she found her at church."

"It didn't turn out well?"

"He's a landscape photographer. He doesn't even take pictures of people. And she kept talking and talking and talking. He was thrilled when he remembered he had an appointment."

"Should I say now that her heart's in the right place?" She couldn't help but smile. "You said you have three unmarried brothers, but you've only mentioned two here. That means someone has gone unscathed."

"Only because he doesn't live in the state. I'm surprised

she didn't find someone on an online dating service, though, and try to fix him up. Please do *not* suggest it to her. And actually, Mark—my out-of-state brother—is in a truck right now headed up the highway, back to Alaska. Mom and Dad don't know that yet. All of us will be here, and all of us will be vulnerable to Mom. The only one that's safe is Adam, and that's because he found Holly."

Rachel couldn't help laughing. This family was so different from her own. "My parents did try to fix my brother up once. The best they seemed to be able to do was the daughter of someone who owned a women's clothing store chain. They thought it might be a great dynasty to combine the two."

"He clearly did not marry that woman."

"She was actually secretly engaged to someone whom her parents did not find suitable. She eloped before their scheduled date. Dreams of a dynasty destroyed. Mother and Father moved on to other business matters and left him alone."

"They didn't try to fix you up? Make you part of a dynasty?"

Sometimes she wished they would have. At least it would have meant she had value to them in some way. "Even though my mother works at my father's side, she's more his assistant than she is part of management. Women in my parents' world don't *make* dynasties. They plan elaborate dinner parties and elegant events. They dress well and make their men look good. But they don't run businesses." She stared out the window. "They couldn't match me up because they'd be selling a future role in the company. That belonged to my brother, not to me in any way."

He reached over, took her hand in his, and gently

squeezed it. Noah did it out of kindness, but it made her heart sing. She liked this man entirely too much. She hoped that some negative qualities of his personality or lifestyle appeared so she could focus on those and forget him easily when she left.

They arrived at the rental car company and got out of the cab. Noah paid the taxi driver, and she noticed him sliding in some extra for Zeke. Rachel stood beside Noah as he took care of the car rental process. When the question arose about any other drivers of the vehicle, he asked her, "Rachel, do you want to be able to drive the car?"

"I haven't driven a car in years, Noah. You would only want me to do that in a dire emergency." The clerk behind the counter's eyes widened, and she got the feeling that the rental company was grateful she declined his offer.

She held her hand over her mouth as she yawned. It would take a few days to recover from all the walking and terror of being out in the wilderness. She loaded her suitcase into the car's trunk, and Noah tossed in his backpack and ice chest. They all settled into the car with Zeke in the backseat, and he drove off.

After a stop at a store for a new phone, life started to feel a little more normal. Then she remembered that she was driving into a practical joke with her pilot and his dog, and normal seemed far away.

CHAPTER TWELVE

"You said it wasn't a very long flight from Anchorage to Kenai—"

Noah turned onto the highway. "About twenty minutes or so. Depending on the weather."

"Is the drive about twice that?"

He laughed. "It might be somewhere like in Kansas. Here in Alaska, we have to drive around large bodies of water and mountains. It's about a three-hour drive."

Her head whipped around. "Are you kidding?"

"No. But it's a beautiful drive. I haven't made it for a while. It's different from the ground. During the first part of the drive, we're close to the water. Then we'll be tucked in among trees."

"Let me know if you see any wildlife, especially bears. I'd like to take a picture of one."

Should he tell her? He glanced over at the woman beside him. He had a feeling she could handle almost anything. "Rachel, probably the closest you will ever be to a bear was when we were walking out of Petersville."

"Excuse me? Are you telling me that there were actual bears, not just bear tracks?"

"I didn't tell you then because I thought you might shriek and catch their attention. Or run. Both of which are bad things. There was a mama and two cubs on the edge of the hill we went down the first day. I hoped that when we moved out of sight, we might be out of scent range as well."

Rachel nodded, but she didn't say a word for a while. "I'm not much of a shrieker, you know?"

"Is anyone absolutely not a shrieker when they see three bears nearby, and there's no fence between you and them, like at the zoo?"

She raised and lowered her shoulders in a shrug. "It's possible you have a valid point." She sighed. "I do wish I had a photo of them, though."

Noah patted his pants pocket. "I snapped a photo in the seconds that we had before we went down the hill. I forgot about it, but you can check to see if what I took is any good." He reached into his pocket, pulled out his phone, and handed it to her, also giving her the code to open it.

Out of the corner of his eye, he watched her scrolling and then stop. "It isn't a great photo, but I can tell that's a brown spot with two small ones beside it. Are these the bears?"

He glanced at the phone. "Yep."

"You were wise not to say anything. I can tell even here that brown bears are big." She returned his phone. "I didn't scream just now. Have I passed some sort of new-to-Alaska test?"

He chuckled. "I think you have."

They drove along in silence for a while. Noah kept running through the plan for when they greeted his mother. This would be short, and Rachel should be able to catch a flight out of Kenai tomorrow morning, maybe even today. She'd go back home to her life in Arlington, whatever that included at this point. They'd only known each other for a few days, but he'd miss her. They'd been together so many hours every day that it must have sped up their friendship. He wondered if it could have actually become something more than friendship if she lived closer than the other side of the country.

He glanced over at her as he was about to ask what she might like for lunch and saw her fast asleep. He might be used to hiking and being in the outdoors, but his passenger was not.

When they neared Soldotna, he reached over and nudged her arm to wake her up. Pulling up to a restaurant he'd often stopped at, he said, "I've been putting off calling Mom to tell her that I'm on my way. She's going to be concerned about the reason why I'm home from my vacation early."

"Do you want to tell her about me or maybe just that you have good news?"

"Good news. Very good plan. This should work."

He dialed his mom's number. "Mom? I'm going to be home from vacation a little bit early, and I brought a guest with me."

Rachel nervously smiled. He'd asked a lot of her.

"No, I'm fine. I'm not injured at all. My plane had a little bit of a problem, but it's running well now. We'll be pulling up to the house in about an hour." He wrapped up the call promising to let her know if his plans changed.

~

As they drove, the number of buildings beside the road grew more dense, signaling their entrance into Kenai. This would be a practical joke that the family would never forget. Thinking about the reveal made him want to chuckle. Then his mind flashed over all the things that could go wrong, and he wanted to pull the car to the side of the road and tell Rachel that he'd made a mistake, that this was the dumbest idea he'd ever had in his life. Unfortunately—or fortunately, depending on how you looked at it—remembering his family's sense of fun overrode his desire for self-preservation.

Rachel sat beside him, staring out the side window.

"Are you having second thoughts? Anyone breathing probably would."

She turned to him with a sad smile. This hadn't been her best day, and he needed to remember that. He had no right to intrude on this time of her life for something like this.

"Rachel, I'm so sorry about what happened earlier."

If they drove directly to the airport in Kenai, she'd be able to get a commercial flight and probably still connect with one out of Anchorage today. She could be home in Virginia by tomorrow morning. He didn't know if it would help her family situation to be there in person or not. He'd never experienced anything like that.

As he was about to offer her that option, she spoke. "I'm sad about the end of the dream. All my life, I have wanted to run this business, even though I knew my brother would almost certainly be the one to do it. I have tried to prove myself to my parents, ever since I figured out that I was somehow less than my brother in their eyes. I didn't truly grasp that until I was a teenager."

"If you want to go home, I can get you to the airport now. It should be pretty easy to get a flight home." He glanced over at her as he finished the sentence, and she turned toward him. He wasn't sure he'd ever seen eyes that sad before.

"I know it's just a job, but it's a situation where life as you thought it was—or at least as you wanted it to be—doesn't exist. I think it's a little like a divorce."

She turned to stare out the front window blankly, and he doubted she had any idea what they were driving past. Before he could offer any other suggestions, she said, "I appreciate the offer, Noah." She looked back at him again. "But I don't have much to go back to. I'll need to help with the sale. It's the right thing to do. But I won't be ready to do that for a few days, anyway." She forced a smile, her cheeks rising with the appearance of happiness, but the result came out grim when combined with the rest of her expression.

He reached over and held her hand. "Probably the worst thing people can say is that it's going to be all right. You're one of the strongest people I know. Look at what you just survived."

"I did do okay, didn't I?"

He grinned. "You did better than okay. You could have sat on the ground and cried or curled up in a ball because you were so afraid. And I wouldn't have blamed you. We were in a situation that you would never experience where you come from."

"So true."

As he started to let go of her hand, he realized something very important. "Rachel, we're supposed to be married, and you don't have a ring."

She held up her left hand, turning it from side to side. "A ring would cost a lot, Noah."

He cringed at the thought of what it must cost for a diamond and gold, and it was just for a joke.

"We could stop at the drugstore and see if they have play jewelry for kids," she suggested. "If no one looks closely, it might pass for the real thing."

"I like that idea." He slowed the car a few minutes later and pulled into the parking lot in front of a drugstore. "Let's see what we can find."

Inside the store, they headed straight for the toys. Rachel picked up a package of play jewelry and flipped it around in her hand. "There is no way that this ring is fitting on my finger. Maybe my pinky, but that doesn't help."

"My thought exactly. It wouldn't even fit on my pinky." He turned in a circle, slowly checking out the signs above the aisles. "Nothing jumps right out at me, Rachel. Do you have any other ideas? Mom's going to send out the cavalry for us if we don't get there in the next hour."

"We could go to a jewelry store, and I—"

"I will not let my fiancée, scratch that, *wife*, pay for her own ring. It's a matter of pride for me to buy the ring." He held up one hand to stop her remarks. "I know that sounds old-fashioned and silly, especially when you consider this isn't a real marriage."

She shrugged. "I actually thought it was kind of sweet. Chivalry isn't necessarily a bad thing. But it doesn't solve our problem, because you need to pay for possible airplane repairs, and you already paid to fly a mechanic out twice to work on your plane." She looked around them, hoping for some sort of inspiration. "Let's walk up and down the aisles of the store to see if something jumps out at us, something we haven't thought of already that would make sense as a ring."

After they'd walked the aisles, Rachel said, "This isn't going to work, Noah. Unless you have visions of carving a candle into a ring shape or painting it on with makeup, I don't think there are any options here. Let me finish the suggestion that I started a few minutes ago. Having a memento of Alaska would be great. What if I bought a ring for myself, not as a wedding band, but just a souvenir?" She watched him, almost daring him to speak. "It would be a ring that I would continue to wear after I go home, and I would always remember this time here. How does that sound?"

He put his hand on his chest. "My masculinity is slightly wounded, but I think I'll get over it. That sounds like the best plan. My ideas were limited to sausage and cheese, and unless edible rings become all the rage, that won't work."

Rachel grinned, and it made his heart happy. *Do not go there, Noah O'Connell.*

After quickly checking her phone, Rachel found a jewelry store with good reviews not too far away. They arrived moments before it was ready to close, but unsurprisingly, the salesperson was happy to wait on them.

"Are you shopping for a diamond ring?" The saleswoman glanced first at Rachel and then over at Noah.

Rachel felt the heat rise on her face. "No, ma'am. I want a ring to remind me of my trip to Alaska. Do you have anything that would be appropriate for that? Not too expensive, a small ring."

The woman studied the cases for a moment and pulled out a tray of rings that were very unique. Rachel had never seen anything like them. "These are gold nugget rings," explained the saleswoman. "We start with a gold ring that's plain, and we solder on actual gold nuggets that are found in streams in Alaska. Each ring is one-of-a-kind, and it's unlikely you'll find this ring style anywhere else."

The rings were all covered in tiny pieces of gold. "They're beautiful! The question is where to start."

The woman laughed, obviously pleased that she had found the right thing for her customer.

Rachel slipped one ring out of the ring tray and tried it on her hand. When she put it on the finger reserved in America for a wedding ring, the woman interrupted.

"Wouldn't this be something worn on the right hand?" She once again looked from Rachel to Noah.

Rachel glanced over at Noah. "No, I think I'm going to wear this one on my left hand for a while. What do you think, honey?" She looked up at her fake husband-to-be and batted her eyelashes.

Clearly taken aback for a moment, he tensed up before seeming to realize she was playing the game. "That's a pretty one, dear. I might like this one better. What do you think?" He held up the ring that had been her second choice when she'd seen the tray.

She pulled off the first ring and set it down then reached her hand toward him, daring him with her eyes to put a ring on her wedding ring finger. Grinning, he did, and as soon as he slipped it on, she knew it was right. A delicate swirl of gold was enhanced with tiny gold nuggets. "It's beautiful. I've never seen anything like this." She held her hand out in front of her. Smiling at the woman, she said, "This is the one I'd like." She slid it around on her finger. "It seems to fit okay, maybe a little bit loose."

The woman reached out to check the fit herself. "If you are considering moving the ring to your right hand and you're right-handed, then that hand probably has larger size fingers because you use it so much. Slip it off and try it there."

Rachel hesitated for half a second. It was silly, but it felt like a betrayal to move the ring from her wedding ring finger to her right hand. But it was a smart suggestion, and she did as the saleswoman had instructed.

The ring fit perfectly.

"If we can take off the tag, this is the one I want. Nice choice, Noah!"

When the woman walked away to take care of the sale, Rachel leaned over and whispered to Noah, "I really do like that ring. And now you can tell your mother you chose it."

He smiled. "She'll like that. She likes anything with a hint of romance."

"Then she should be thrilled about our whirlwind romance."

The saleswoman walked toward them with the ring in a box. "Did I hear you say romance?"

This was a small town, and the fewer people who thought the two of them had an actual romance the better. "Your store does have an air of romance. I'm sure people enjoy buying their wedding rings from you."

That seemed to satisfy the woman because she did not pursue the question any further.

Driving away, Rachel admired the ring on her hand. The weight on that finger felt unexpectedly good and solid.

"I keep feeling like I'm going to meet the in-laws for the first time. But I've met your mother, and she *is* responsible for us being a couple." She used air quotes around the last word.

"Mom doesn't hold back at any point, so you met the real Mrs. O'Connell already. Dad, he's a nice guy. He somehow managed to raise five boys who turned out right."

Rachel's nervousness ratcheted up a few notches when he turned off the highway and started driving down side streets that were becoming more and more like an average neighborhood.

"At least it'll just be them at home. We can play the joke on Mom, explain it all, and tell my brothers about it and laugh later. No harm done."

"I'm glad. Because I kind of liked your mom."

"It's clear that she liked you too since she threw you at her youngest son."

Noah turned right onto a residential street and slowed about halfway down the block.

Rachel was about to ask which house his parents owned when she noticed a mailbox elaborately painted with a variety of flowers further down the street. As they drew closer, she saw a decorative flag in the front yard that said "Spring" and had a bouquet of flowers on it, this time tulips. Expecting Noah to continue and pull into the driveway, she was surprised when he stopped before that house and pulled to the side of the road.

"This may not be as simple as I'd planned. That car in the driveway belongs to my brother Jack. If someone's visiting, this could be more complicated than I'd expected." As he put the car in reverse, his mother stepped out onto the front porch and came down the sidewalk toward the mailbox.

"Get down!" He pushed on the top of her head.

As she sank below the dashboard, she saw his mother looking directly at them. The older woman's face lit up in a smile.

"Noah, it's too late."

He peered up over the dash. "Rats! She's on her way over here. Sit up straight. If she asks, you were looking for something."

"Yes," she muttered. "My sanity."

He chuckled. "I heard that."

She started to formulate a new plan. They could say they had become friends.

His mother knocked on the driver's side window.

When Noah rolled the window down, Rachel waved at her. "It's nice to see you again, Mrs. O'Connell."

Zeke woofed from the backseat.

His mother's eyes widened. She glanced from Rachel to her son and back to him, then they fastened on the gold glittering on Rachel's left hand.

She pointed and sputtered, "Wh-wh-what is that?"

This was the moment. Rachel's last comment about sanity came to mind. She was right. He opened his mouth to explain her presence, his mind whirling for a plausible and truthful excuse, when his dad stepped out onto the front porch.

He called out to his wife, and she turned toward him and shouted, "Noah got engaged!"

"What?" he shouted back. Then his brother joined his dad on the front step.

"Mom, why don't we park the car and all go inside?"

She stepped back, gave the car one more glance, and hurried toward the house, no doubt to tell the family there about the ring on Rachel's hand.

As they pulled into the driveway beside his brother's car, Rachel said, "Let the games begin?"

"My plan is to let this run a couple of hours. Then it will be contained to just my parents. And Jack."

She put her hand over his on the steering wheel. "They'll laugh, right?"

In a low voice, he said, "I hope so. My family loves a practical joke. This one should win practical joke of the year, don't you think?"

Rachel popped open the car door. "I think you may win practical joke of the decade."

As they walked over to Noah's family, with Zeke leading the way, Rachel was relieved to find that his parents and brother seemed excited but not overwrought. If she'd brought a fiancé or husband home to *her* parents . . . it wouldn't have been pretty. She'd always assumed that she didn't like surprises because her parents didn't. Surprises had a negative connotation for her. But if this played out the way Noah hoped it would, that might change her mind.

His mother didn't wait for them to get to the front porch. She hurried the last few steps and hugged Rachel for a long moment then released her. "Welcome to the family, Rachel."

The hug felt like a balm to her spirit. "It's good to be here, Mrs. O'Connell."

His mother patted her on the arm and said, "We'll be happy to welcome you to the family."

Mrs. O'Connell turned toward Noah. "She *is* your fiancée, isn't she?"

Rachel spared him the lie. She held up her left hand. "Noah helped me choose the ring. And he slid it on my finger." All true. He reached his arm around her and pulled her next to him. She knew it was part of the act, but she enjoyed being close to him nevertheless.

"Then first, please call me Mom."

"Mom, she already has a mother. Could she call you by your first name?"

Rachel thought about it for all of three seconds before she said, "I'd actually like to call you Mom."

His mother smiled broadly.

"So you're engaged. And I brought you together. I must admit that it wasn't very many days ago—"

"Four," Noah said.

His mother paused.

His dad asked, "Four days, son?"

Jack added, "Yeah, bro, are you sure about this? Do you really want to be engaged to someone after only four days?"

Noah turned toward Rachel with a faux-loving expression on his face. She had to bite her lip to not laugh because it was so over-the-top. "We knew almost instantly, didn't we, Rachel?"

"Love at first sight always seemed elusive to me, but now I believe in it." That was so saccharine sweet that she could barely finish saying the words.

His mother said, "Let's all go inside. It's still a little chilly out here."

After letting Zeke out in the fenced backyard, they settled in the living room, and Rachel noticed how flower-free the room was. She and Noah sat side by side on the loveseat, steered there by his mother. His dad had chosen a large recliner, his brother a smaller chair, and his mother sat on the corner of the larger sofa. All of the furniture was either a medium-gray color or a bold plaid in black, white, and gray. His mother wore the only flowers in the room with a floral print top, jeans with flowers embroidered on them, and sneakers that appeared to have daisies painted on them.

His father said, "What happened with your 170?"

It amazed Rachel that she actually knew he was talking about an airplane. A week ago she wouldn't have had any idea.

Mrs. O'Connell asked, "Yes, Noah, tell us what happened to your plane. We have a lot of time, I'm sure, to enjoy you and Rachel as an engaged couple."

Noah turned to Rachel and raised one eyebrow. Which direction would he choose? Talk about the plane incident or their "marriage"? He either wimped out or decided to bide his time and build up to the high point of his practical joke.

"The story begins with how we met. Rachel, why don't you explain how that happened?" He turned and glared at his mother.

Rachel bit her lip to keep from laughing. After composing herself, she began their story. "I met your mother at the airport, and she asked me to play a practical joke on you by speaking with an Irish accent. I can because my family has an Irish heritage, and I've been to Ireland numerous times."

Jack grinned. "Tell me more." His features reminded her some of Noah's, but he had brown hair instead of blond. He had a rugged appearance that told her that, like Noah, he could probably survive in the wilds. Still grinning, he sat back with his arms crossed, clearly enjoying the show.

"I'd been tricked into believing an Irish accent."

"Now, Noah, don't exaggerate." Mrs. O'Connell raised her eyebrows at her son. "I didn't do anything bad. She would say a line or two and get in your airplane. I thought you'd spend about an hour together, tops, and never see each other again." She once again studied them. "Did you decide to have dinner with her when you got to Talkeetna?" She clearly enjoyed hearing the story of how her son had fallen in love with the woman she'd matched him with, even though it shouldn't have been more than a joke.

"Yes. But not that day. We actually had more of an adventure. I've been flying that plane for a few months and had no problems. It had been thoroughly checked out, but I lost power between here and Talkeetna."

His mother gasped and put her hand on her chest. His brother and father leaned forward, waiting to hear the rest of the story. He explained the emergency landing. "Thank God, Rachel spotted the runway."

"I just wish I'd spotted one closer to civilization."

His dad said, "When you were all still fairly young, we went as a family to the area around Mt. McKinley. I think we drove the road toward Petersville, but had to turn around when the motor home we'd borrowed couldn't drive any further."

Jack said, "I remember that we did drive there, and we found old gold mines, but not much else."

Noah agreed. "Until a few days ago, that's all I knew about it too."

Rachel pictured the landscape in her mind. "It's beautiful. It's wild, but it's peaceful and quiet in a way I'd never experienced before. Once we found the road, we could walk more easily, although it was muddy and we had to cross raging rivers—"

His dad chuckled. "Someone from the city would think that any Alaskan adventure was extreme. Raging rivers?"

Noah shook his head. "*Raging* rivers. It's spring, and there was a whole lot of water. We crossed, what was it, four, Rachel?"

She nodded. "I lost count, but I believe so."

"Having only light, late-season snow saved us. Rachel definitely hadn't packed for hiking through snow."

His mother leaned back on the sofa. "Oh my! Are you both okay? You were apparently rescued."

"We're fine, Mom. Still a little bit tired. But we're grateful, aren't we, honey?" He turned toward her and winked his right eye so no one else would see. "Nothing changed except our hearts."

Rachel wasn't sure whether to gag or roll off the sofa laughing. "Nothing too bad other than my blisters. Which do seem to be healing nicely."

His mother gave a long, swoon-worthy sigh. "That's lovely. Have you set a date for the wedding?"

Rachel twisted the ring on her finger while she waited for Noah to answer. He'd set them on this path, so it was up to him to pull off the joke.

"Rachel and I realized, why wait? When you've found the right one, you know it."

"So I need to quickly plan a wedding?"

Rachel could see the wheels spinning in his mother's mind as she thought of her dream wedding for Noah. She was almost disappointed that she didn't have one for the lady to plan. Almost. She had too much on her plate right now to even consider anything beyond work and family. Her own family.

Noah took Rachel's hand in his and held it up. "Mom, this is a wedding ring, not an engagement ring."

She rose to her feet. "You're married!" She walked across the room, turned, and walked back. Then stopped and stared at her son. "Could we do another ceremony?"

Noah shook his head. "I don't see any reason for that, do you, honeybun?"

Rachel covered her mouth with her hand to hide the laughter and coughed. Clearing her throat, she said, "Once you're married, I don't see any reason for another ceremony. We don't need all those things, do we, snuggle bunny?"

This time, she could see Noah fighting laughter. Served him right.

His mother stood there, staring at the two of them with her mouth hanging open. Then she turned and headed away from them. "I'm going to get started on dinner. No wedding to plan?" She muttered as she walked away, shaking her head.

Rachel patted Noah on the knee, then stood. "I think I'll go see if she needs any help in the kitchen." She headed that direction.

Noah knew that the kitchen was the last place his lovely wife should be, both for the reason that she couldn't cook and because his mother might be inclined to grill her to see what other information she could learn.

His dad stood. "She seems like a lovely girl, Noah. I hope you're happy together. It is a little sudden, though, son." He also walked away. "I'm going to finish up a project in my shop, if either of you would like to join me later."

When everyone had cleared the room except for Jack and Noah, Jack came over and sat down beside him. Looking around the room as though he were checking to make sure they were unobserved, his brother said, "Nicely played, brother."

Noah wondered if he should ask what his brother meant,

but he wasn't stupid. Jack had figured it out. "What gave me away?"

"Honeybun?"

Noah grinned. "I went too far, didn't I?"

His brother laughed. He glanced around again before adding, "Mom and Dad are buying it. I guess I know you better. I don't think you would call a girl honeybun no matter how much you were in love with her."

Noah smacked Jack lightly on the arm.

"I will say that she's beautiful and she seems very nice. And she looks rather taken with you. She must be to go along with this farce of yours."

"She's had a lot going on with her family lately." Noah explained about Talkeetna, Rachel's parents, and the family business. "When she didn't seem to want to go right home, this idea came to mind. I think she's happy to have a little bit of fun in her life."

"How long will you continue this?"

Noah shifted in his seat. "Well, I thought it would be Mom and Dad here alone, and it would be very simple. After dinner, I'd confess. Very simple." He dusted his hands together as though he was brushing it off.

"I'm not telling anyone."

"Yeah. Maybe it will still work."

His mother called from the kitchen, "Noah, honey!" He cringed when she used his name and 'honey' in the same sentence. All of them did. "Your bride is doing a good job here in the kitchen!"

"Mom must be helping her. Rachel will be the first to tell you she doesn't know how to cook." Noah cringed. "The steaks the first night? Shoe leather."

"How did you cook those steaks?" Jack asked. "Over an

open fire?"

"No. We actually found a cabin that had a propane stove the first night."

Jack laughed. "And you and I both know that cooking on propane isn't the same. It's hotter."

"True. She did cook them, though. That's Rachel. She does whatever she needs to do." Noah thought about the plan for his practical joke. It was *almost* going the way he'd expected. "I think it will work to let Mom simmer during dinner, to think about all the flowers she didn't get to use in a wedding—"

His brother chuckled.

"And lament the fact that she did not get to go wedding dress shopping with Rachel." Noah smacked his brother on the arm. "Why don't you and I go out and see if Dad could use some help?"

They both stood, and Jack said, "I'm looking forward to tomorrow's lunch. Mom always does an amazing Saturday lunch. I think she mentioned something about a roast."

"My favorite."

His mother stepped out of the kitchen with her phone in her hand. Rachel followed her with a shocked expression on her face.

"I've called your brothers, and they'll all be here for lunch tomorrow, so they can meet your wife. Except Mark, of course."

His mother went back to the kitchen and Rachel followed, giving him an expression that said, "Help!"

Noah watched them, wondering what if anything he should do right now.

"I think your plans just changed."

"I should wait until everyone's here tomorrow. And I

probably need to wait until after lunch to tell her, or it might ruin the whole thing."

His brother laughed. "For you *and* for me. Yes, please wait, so that I can enjoy lunch. Then I'm going to head back out on the road. I have a lot of photos I want to take before spring and summer turn to colder weather."

As they went out the back door and toward the shed that their father used for his woodworking, Noah asked, "So why are you at Mom and Dad's today?"

"I'm here to photograph the Kenai River. A friend is doing an article on salmon fishing, and he wanted to add a photo of the river when it isn't salmon season."

When they got to the shed, Noah stopped. "Are you enjoying life since you sold your jewelry store?"

"I grew very tired of having to be there every day when I wanted to be outside taking photos of landscapes and animals."

"You stuck it out for quite a while as you waited for your photography business to grow." He clapped his brother on the back. "I know that wasn't easy."

"I'm enjoying my freedom, and I think I'm going to move permanently to Homer. No matter how many times I visit, Homer calls me back."

Noah sighed, then he reached for the doorknob. "Mountains, ocean, forests. Homer 's beautiful. You're making a living with your photography?" He paused. "Listen to me. I sound like Mom or Dad asking about your money."

Jack laughed. "I'm doing well. I'm not going to buy a castle tomorrow, but it's growing all the time. I've seen some amazing scenery. Last week, I took a boat over to Seldovia and got some amazing photos of humpback whales."

Noah turned the knob and started to push the door open.

"Up by Petersville, where Rachel and I were, it's gorgeous. When the snow is all gone, and the roads are dried out, you might want to take a trek up there to get some photos. You can actually see all of Mount McKinley on a clear day. Stunning."

They walked into the shop.

His dad said, "Your wife *is* stunning."

"I was talking about McKinley. But she is pretty, isn't she?"

"She is that, son."

After a dinner that was surprisingly good, considering Rachel had been involved in its making, they left amid hugs and handshakes and promises to return tomorrow for lunch at noon sharp. Driving away in the rental car with Zeke again in the backseat, Rachel asked, "I've only just realized that you must have a car here. You live in Kenai, right?"

Noah turned onto the highway and the direction of his home. "Yes to both."

"And we haven't returned the rental car yet because?"

He could feel her eyes watching him. Noah put on the signal to make a left turn. "Because I paid for the rental for a full day and would not save any money by returning it earlier." He didn't mention that he hadn't figured out yet how to return the car if she wouldn't drive it back. He'd have to ask his dad because he didn't want to push someone to drive who was nervous about it. That might be a bad idea.

He thought through their sleeping arrangements tonight. He'd give her the bed in his bedroom and take the sofa, as painful as that thought was.

They pulled up to his apartment building, a somewhat older two-story unit he'd gotten for a great rental rate. As a bachelor, he really hadn't cared where he lived as long as it was safe, clean, and not far from the airport he flew out of. Of course, his mother had decorated. Again, he didn't really care. She knew that not one of the men in her life wanted flowers around them in the decor. So, he'd felt confident turning it over to her. But he would have been okay with simple used furniture instead of the new stuff she bought him. That probably just made him a regular guy.

He clipped on Zeke's leash, and they walked up the stairs to the second story corner unit.

"Should I expect a bachelor dump? My brother always had someone come in to clean. It had a sterile, not lived-in appearance. But tidy. Is this going to be . . . bachelor scary?"

She had a way of making him laugh. She had such a fun way of seeing the world for someone whose life hadn't included a whole lot of fun. He was grateful that her sense of humor had not been beaten out of her, both for her sake and for his as long as he was around her.

They reached his unit, and he opened the door, letting it swing wide and stepping back so that Rachel could enter first.

"Wow, Noah. I expected, I don't know, messiness and a sofa that had the corner missing because Zeke used it for a snack one day—and maybe a bit of a locker-room smell. But this." She waved her hand at the room.

Noah closed the door behind them. At that moment, Rachel spotted the one floral piece in the room, a throw pillow on the sofa. It was tasteful, and he'd been able to live with it, but the gray and white flowers with a little hint of yellow definitely showed his mother's hand in the decorating.

She held up the pillow with a questioning expression on her face.

"You're right. Mom did it."

She wandered from the bedroom to the bathroom and ended up in the kitchen. Then she whipped around and leaned against the kitchen island as though she'd just realized something important. "One bedroom?"

"Don't worry. I'm not going to make you share a bed with me again."

Her face blushed a pretty pink.

He pointed at the sofa. "This is my bed for tonight." He wished he'd done a sitting test on the sofa before paying for it. Instead, his mother had simply bought what suited the design and the small size of his apartment.

"Noah." She shook her head from side to side. "You're taller than that sofa is long, aren't you?"

He looked down at the sofa that was barely bigger than a loveseat. "If it's too small for me, I'll sleep on the floor. After what we've been through, having a warm, safe place with heat, indoor plumbing, and snacks available sounds like luxurious living. I'll be fine."

Unfortunately, this sofa probably wouldn't give him a good night's sleep, which was something he really wanted right now. He hadn't said anything to anyone, but their adventure had left him with some sore muscles too.

Rachel stood where she was. When he was about to ask what was wrong, she said, "I feel really guilty about leaving you on that sofa. It's too short. That isn't fair. I know we aren't on our survival adventure anymore, but we're trying to survive your joke. We can figure something else out."

It made his heart happy that Rachel cared about his well-being. "There's one thing you didn't notice when you peered into the bedroom."

Her eyebrows rose.

"It's a twin bed. Mom wanted me to get a bigger bed, but I saw no need, and decided to save the money." He sat and patted the sofa cushion beside him. The firm cushion barely moved. "This is my bed for the night."

Then an idea occurred to him. He went over to his backpack, which he'd stowed against the wall, expecting to unpack it tomorrow or whenever this marriage ended. He untied the sleeping pad from above the sleeping bag and held it up.

Rachel's face lit up, then she frowned. "But is the sofa that bad?"

He turned and stared at the largest piece of furniture in the room. "Yeah, it is. I think I'm going to replace it very soon."

Rachel pursed her lips. "You know, I could go to a hotel. No one would ever know. I could come back in the morning, and it's all good. Right?"

He laughed. "I can tell that we come from different kinds of families, Rachel. Your family doesn't drop by, does it?"

"I don't think they have ever dropped by. I'm not even sure that my mother and father know where I live, other than an address in a file, of course."

Noah felt sorry for her. He had such a great family. It did seem, though, that she and David would have a good relationship going forward. Even if they hadn't when they were younger, at least they could be close when they were older. He had a feeling that would mean a lot to her.

CHAPTER THIRTEEN

The next morning, Noah went into the kitchen to make coffee, rubbing his back as he did. "I want to give you a warning. The reason I asked you to sleep here last night was because, with my family, someone could knock on that door at any time."

Rachel gave him a look that said she didn't believe they would show up. She crossed the room and opened the door. "I don't recognize anybody out there. Maybe you're wrong."

She closed the door and joined him in the kitchen. Then she opened up cupboards and sorted through them until she found mugs and set them on the counter.

"Mine's the mug with the cartoon characters on it."

She raised one eyebrow and then traded one mug on the counter for one in the cupboard that had characters from a popular cartoon about twenty years ago.

"Hey, they're still cute."

Grinning, she set it on the counter.

After half of a mug of coffee, Rachel said, "I'm going to go take a nice hot shower. And then I'm going to come out and search on my phone for a nearby hotel."

"The practical joke is wrapping up today at lunch, remember?"

She shook her head. "Noah, I usually keep to a pretty tight schedule. I have to with my work." She paused. "I *had* to. Past tense. But nothing, and I do mean *nothing* has gone according to plan since I stepped off that airplane in Anchorage earlier this week. My guess is that we've got at least one more night before this farce comes to an end." At that, she set down her mug, walked into the bedroom, and came back out with her arms filled with everything she'd need to shower and dress.

When he heard the bathroom door click to lock, he set down his mug. This was a strange situation. He was married but not. Every day spent with his "wife" made him like her more. She was leaving, probably not to return until she came to spend more time with her brother and his upcoming baby. A big-city girl like her would want nothing to do with a pilot living in Kenai, Alaska. This whole situation kept getting more difficult. He'd make sure the big reveal came during lunch.

Rachel sat on the sofa and scrolled through her phone while Noah was in the shower. In the ten minutes that took, her backside started to get sore. This piece of furniture truly was more decorative than functional. He came out and sat down on the sofa next to her, wincing as he did.

Rachel looked at him. "We could spend some time this morning shopping for a better sofa for you. I can tell that your mother chose all of this because it's decorated very much like her house. What color do you like best?"

He shifted on the sofa as though he were trying to get comfortable and couldn't. "You're right. She chose everything in here. The one thing that I put my foot down about was the twin bed, and that seems to have been a mistake."

She wasn't sure it was truly a mistake. They were no longer in a tense emergency situation, and sharing a bed with Noah didn't sound like a good plan.

"I'm not sure I'll be staying in Kenai much longer, anyway."

"What?" She turned toward him. "Are you leaving Alaska?"

"I can't imagine ever living somewhere else again. I've done that, and I came back. No, the airline that I fly for keeps asking me to move to Anchorage. They need someone who's there. I always said no in the past, but now that Adam and Holly are near there and they have the twins, it's more appealing. I haven't decided. The airline messages me about it every day, very nicely asking me to please reconsider. There were three texts from them when we got service again in Talkeetna."

She stood. "I'm not sure who would want this sofa, but it is pretty. Maybe there are some people who wouldn't notice how uncomfortable it is."

Zeke ran to the door and then someone knocked.

Noah smirked. "If that isn't one of my family members, I will be stunned. Zeke is wagging his tail." He stood, wincing a bit as he rose, and went over to the door.

"Surprise!"

Rachel recognized his mother's voice. Thinking that

maybe she'd brought over a meal for the newlyweds, she stood and walked over so that she could thank her.

When she was almost there, his dad said, "Help me get this bed out of the truck, son. Jack and Andy will take one end. You and I can get the other."

Rachel stopped in her tracks. Noah had a panicked expression.

As if sensing their confusion, his mother added, "I know you have a twin bed, Noah, but there's such a thing as too much closeness when you're married. I'm sure that a queen bed will fit in that room very nicely."

A wave of panic swept over his face. The joke had gotten far more complicated. Now he'd have to repay them for a bed.

Rachel grinned and shrugged.

Noah snapped Zeke's leash onto him and handed it to Rachel before following his father down the stairs.

His mother stepped into the apartment with a big bag in her hands and handed it to Rachel. "I knew he wouldn't have any linens for the new bed, so I bought a set of sheets, a blanket, and comforter with a beautiful floral pattern."

Rachel accepted the bag from her and peered inside.

Jack and Andy were standing next to his dad's pickup, Jack with a silly grin on his face because he knew the true story.

As soon as Noah arrived, Andy shook his hand, clapped him on the back, and then brought him in for a hug. Stepping back, he said, "Congratulations, Noah! This is a surprise, isn't it?"

Jack apparently couldn't resist making a comment. "Surprise after surprise, isn't it, Noah?" He smirked.

His brother had obviously been true to his word. Andy didn't have a clue about the true nature of their marriage. They carried the bed frame upstairs and assembled it. On the next trip, they slid the box springs out of the truck, and with two of them on each end, carried it upstairs. Noah was pretty sure two of them alone could have carried it, but they were here to support each other. On the final trip, they brought the mattress and slid it onto the bed. When he saw the empty mattress sitting there and his old twin bed hastily propped against the wall with the sheets still on it, he realized that they had an out for not sleeping on this bed tonight.

Rachel handed him a bag. "Your mom thoughtfully purchased bedding for our new bed."

His mom said, "Why don't the two of you lie down on the bed to see how it feels?"

Rachel's eyes grew wide.

His dad stepped in. Thankfully. "I think we'll let these newlyweds test the bed out on their own." He herded everyone out of the bedroom, but the implications of his father's words had put a blush on Rachel's cheeks.

As his family walked toward the door, Rachel leaned in close and whispered into his ear, "No bed testing."

He whispered back, "Don't worry."

His mother hurried over to the door. "Let's go, everyone. I need to get back and work on lunch. You two are coming, right, Noah and Rachel?"

"We said we'd be there, Mom. Don't worry."

Andy gave him a thumbs up, apparently approving of his choice of bride, but Jack shook his head as he went by.

When Jack walked out of the apartment, he paused a

moment to say in a low voice to his brother, "You're revealing all at lunch, right?"

Noah still felt like he was in shock about the bed. "I'd better. Now I owe Mom and Dad for a brand-new bed that I didn't want or need."

"Then I'll see you at lunch. Oh, and I think Mom mentioned something about Adam bringing Holly and the twins." With that, he gave a wave and went out the door, closing it behind himself.

Noah turned to Rachel. "I am so sorry about all of this."

She burst out laughing. "This is the most fun I've had in years. Maybe ever. I like your family."

Noah gave a wry smile. "They like my new wife as well."

She laughed again. "Let's go return that rental car and get your truck."

"Oh no! I should have had one of my brothers stay to help!"

"You can drive."

"Rachel, my truck is parked in this lot. It's right out front. Someone needs to drive my truck over to the car rental place. You're going to have to follow me in it."

CHAPTER FOURTEEN

*R*achel stepped back, waving her hands. "Noah, it's been several years since I've been behind the wheel of a car, and I've never driven a pickup truck. Maybe I could drive the rental car."

"No. Remember how you didn't want to be on the rental car agreement? I can't let you drive it."

"You're right. Well, I've never let a challenge stand in my way." She sighed. "I'm apparently going to drive a truck."

Rachel got behind the wheel of what turned out to not just be a pickup truck, but what Noah called a crew cab pickup—a four-door version with a backseat that made it as long as a riverboat. At least it felt that way as she tried to maneuver it out of the parking lot. She'd never sat this high above other vehicles. Noah had backed it up from the parking space because he'd told her he didn't want to have Rachel scratch *her* sides.

Following him down the road, she held onto the steering wheel with both hands and was grateful for the fact that this area didn't have much traffic. As she'd climbed into the truck, Noah said something about being glad that it wasn't summertime when all the tourists were in town, and both they and locals crowded the rivers fishing for salmon. Ten minutes later, she was pulling into the rental car lot. She'd done it.

After he'd returned the car, they were both in his truck and pulling out, Noah driving now. Rachel said, "I found some places to stay that aren't too far from your apartment or too expensive."

"Rachel, I told you that we would get this resolved today. I'll confess at lunchtime. It's perfect because everyone's there."

"Noah, last night, you had a twin bed. It looked a whole lot better to the outside world than it will now that you have that lovely queen bed, which your mother explained was very comfortable."

"We'll act married when we arrive. Then I'll reveal our joke a while later."

She admired his optimism and hoped it would prove correct.

"Don't worry. Everyone knows we just met. Remember: it's love at first sight."

Rachel watched Noah as he drove toward his parents' house. There was something quite special about him. He cared about his family. He cared about other people.

As they drove, she thought about friends she'd known who had gotten married and their newlywed conversations. "We should do a little more fact-finding between us. It's normal to have talked about our lives. Someone is bound to ask a question, and we won't know the answer to it."

This time, as they neared the house, an SUV was pulling into the driveway. As they parked on the street, a dark-haired woman stepped out of the passenger side of that vehicle and opened the side door to reveal two small, identical girls.

"Didn't you say they were recently married?" Rachel asked. The children looked to be about five or six. "The twins were Holly's from before she married Adam?"

"They were. But the father wanted nothing to do with them once he learned that she was pregnant with twins, so he doesn't have any custody rights. Adam's in the process of officially adopting Abbie and Ivy as his own. The girls, of course, know life from before him, but they quickly began calling him Dad." A man with the same hair color as Noah and similar features stepped around the front of the vehicle and leaned down to kiss his wife.

The O'Connell family home wasn't large. Rachel knew they'd moved here after their children were gone, so they hadn't lived here with five growing boys. Right now, it was packed.

Rachel took a deep breath. She'd survived the crowds in retail during the Christmas season. She could handle this. She put on a smile and prepared to greet Noah's family as his wife. But the already out-of-control situation escalated when they opened the door, and another dog met Zeke with a flurry of barks.

They touched noses and must have agreed to run around the house because they chased each other through the living room and back.

Noah called Zeke in a firm voice. His dog stopped but had an expression on his face that said, "Do you really want me to stop having fun?" Noah went over to him and tugged gently on his collar to take him out the back door. Adam, apparently the owner of the other dog, didn't even have to do that because his dog followed his friend. With both dogs in the backyard, Noah closed the door, turned around, and leaned against it with a weary expression.

What had he done? His mother's simple prank on him had needed some sort of response. His family would expect that once they knew the story. His practical joke had seemed so simple. Pretend to be married for a few hours. He glanced around the house filled with laughter and people, many of them here to celebrate his new marriage to Rachel. She was smiling, but it didn't look like her usual smile. This must be her professional smile to a customer.

He could see into the kitchen from here, and the sheer volume of food was staggering. Abbie and Ivy were in the kitchen, standing on stools, helping his mother, and their mother Holly watched from a few feet away. His mom dipped a spoon into something to taste it and set the spoon aside.

He definitely couldn't tell everyone before or during lunch because his mom would be upset, and it would ruin the meal for everyone. Maybe over dessert. Dessert made people happy. Judging from the two pies Holly had brought and the chocolate frosted cake that his mother had made, there would be a lot of joy in this room.

He straightened and went over to Rachel's side, putting his arm around her and pulling her close. He knew he needed to put on a good front for the family. When she sank into his side with relief, his guilt ratcheted up a few more notches. She'd come to Alaska to find her brother, and it had been a wild ride ever since. She'd be glad to get back to her straightforward life outside of D.C.

"Noah," Adam said, "come over here and explain again about this adventure. Did you really have to make an emergency landing in the wilderness?"

Keeping his arm around Rachel, he led her over to where his older brother sat with Jack and Andy. Andy got up and moved over to sit at the end of the sofa so Noah and Rachel could sit together on the loveseat. It seemed to be their piece of furniture now. He did his best to ignore the word "love" in the furniture's name.

Noah leaned forward with his elbows on his thighs and recounted the story of their emergency landing. Adam was the only other one out of the five O'Connell boys who had a pilot's license.

"So the communications went dead at the same time as the engine?"

"Yes, and I never want to experience that again. Holding on to the heavy airplane and not being able to call for help? I wasn't sure I'd ever see any of you again."

"What about the ELT?"

Noah glanced over at Rachel. No one else had known to ask. He hoped she wasn't too upset by the answer. "The plane didn't crash. I made a controlled landing, so it didn't go off. It's the older version, anyway."

Adam glared at him.

"I know I should update the emergency locator transmitter." He said the full name for Rachel's benefit. "It worked fine when it was tested and seemed to be an unnecessary expense when I bought the plane."

"The older version broadcasts on a rarely monitored frequency. If you do go down in a rougher landing in the future, at least someone will hear the distress call." He sighed. "You must have had the hand of God holding you up in that airplane that day. A dead stick? I've only experienced that in training, and it wasn't fun."

Noah could still feel the airplane in his hands as he struggled to keep it airborne and find a safe place to land.

"The thing is that if Rachel hadn't been with me, I would still have been flying in that general direction, just not planning to land in Talkeetna, and I wouldn't have had a second set of eyes in the airplane. Well, not human eyes. She's the one who spotted the airfield. She'd spotted a road before that, but it had trees on both sides. We might have landed, and walked away from it, but I never would have flown that plane again."

He could feel Rachel's nervousness and tension.

Adam seemed to see it too because he changed the subject as his wife walked over. "On a lighter note, Holly is doing well with her romance novels. She has three out now."

Holly beamed and sat beside Adam. "I'm having fun writing them. The one I'm writing now is about love at first sight." She scooted forward on her seat, smiling happily. "I need to talk to people who fell in love at first sight, so that I get it right."

Noah heard her words, and he was glad she was excited about her project, but he didn't understand the impact of her words until he realized she was looking straight at Rachel. His "wife" hadn't figured it out yet either because she still wore her pasted-on smile.

"Rachel, could I interview you as research for the book?"

Rachel's fair skin turned even paler. She glanced over at Noah. Her eyes said, *save me*. Then she got a determined expression, sat up, took a deep breath, and looked back at Holly. "I'm not sure we actually fell in love at first sight. Would you say that, Noah?"

He laughed at the idea. "She's right, Holly. I did love what turned out to be a fake Irish accent. But everyone in the room knows about that. I wasn't even remotely interested in her until I knew her a little bit."

"What about you, Rachel?"

"I'm the same. He was a pilot taking me to Talkeetna. I came to Alaska to find my brother. And then he became the man I had to rely on to get out of that wilderness. I could help you find your way around a major city, but fording a rushing river was not in my portfolio until this last week."

Nicely handled, Rachel.

CHAPTER FIFTEEN

he men decided to go out to the workshop. About two steps away from her, Noah stopped and turned around. "I'm sorry, Rachel. Would you like to see Dad's new saw?"

She had a hard time fighting a smile. She did respect every craft and art, but she had no personal interest in woodworking. "Go. Enjoy. You can tell me about it later."

With a nod, he turned and trailed his dad and brothers out the back door. The two jubilant dogs barked their greetings and then the door closed. That left her and Holly, whom she barely knew. Holly came over and sat next to her on the loveseat.

Holly said, in a very low voice, "What's the deal with you and Noah?"

At Rachel's surprised expression—she knew she wore one because she could feel it on her face—Holly added, "I know things aren't as Noah has said. What's up?" She motioned toward herself with her hand. "Give."

Rachel grinned. She had a feeling that she and Holly

would get along well as friends. Too bad she was going to be heading back to the East Coast.

How did she phrase this? Noah had told her that Jack had already guessed the truth. If she told Holly, would Holly tell her husband? How far would the truth spread before Noah revealed it?

Holly settled back in her seat. "I have two sisters, and I can read you like you're my third. I hope you really are married to Noah."

They could hear pots and pans in the kitchen. "Are you sure we shouldn't go in and help Mrs. O'Connell with lunch?"

Holly nodded her head with an appreciative expression on her face. "Nice try. But I'm the youngest of the three sisters and the one who isn't easily diverted. Many attempts have been made. You'll have to do better than that."

Rachel laughed. "You want all of it or the short version?"

Holly grinned and leaned forward. "Give me all of it."

"Mrs. O'Connell didn't just introduce us. We met when I was trying to get a flight to Talkeetna where my family believed my brother was."

If anything, Holly leaned forward a little bit more.

"She said her son was flying the direction I wanted to go. The man who was behind the counter knew of him and said he was an excellent pilot. Then she asked if I could speak with an Irish accent."

Holly's brow furrowed. "That's weird. Why would she ask that?"

"He's apparently a sucker for an Irish accent. She knew exactly which buttons to push for a practical joke."

"The O'Connells love practical jokes. They're always harmless, and everyone laughs when they're revealed."

"I'm glad about that. Anyway, I greeted him with an Irish accent. I've been in Ireland many times both for pleasure and for fun. We have extended family that still live there. And even though my family came to America in the mid-1800s, I have an uncle who moved back when I was a kid."

"So she played a joke. You got in the plane and told Noah what happened."

"No. I thought I was going to spend less than an hour with this man and never see him again. I stuck with the Irish accent. My family doesn't have much fun, and it sounded harmless. That all changed when the engine stopped running." She described the landing of the airplane, and Holly's eyes got wider and wider.

"I knew Noah had had some sort of a problem with the plane, but I didn't realize any of this! So you confessed after the accident. And he was angry?"

Rachel thought back to that moment. "I was so scared that I forgot to have an Irish accent. And I don't think he was so much angry as embarrassed that he could be sucked in by my accent. My red hair and fair skin had sealed the deal for him. I apparently remind him of his grandmother."

"That's a little less than romantic." Holly laughed. "You waited to be picked up by a rescue team?"

"You really haven't heard the whole story, have you? We walked out of there and finally found help after two days. I know Noah pretty well at this point. At least I think I do. It's like they say about people who spend time in the trenches. It's a different relationship that you have. It's bonding for life."

"So because of this relationship, you decided to get *married?*" She gave the word emphasis as though she couldn't believe it would happen.

Rachel looked toward the kitchen where she could still hear sounds of pots and pans and water running. "As we flew back to Anchorage, Noah had this genius idea for a practical joke to pay his mom back for the Irish accent."

Holly loudly said, "I knew it!"

His mother said from the kitchen, "Knew what, dear?"

Holly glanced that way, her eyes wide. She whispered, "I add extra cinnamon to apple pies, then they get rave reviews." In a louder voice, she said, "Rachel and I were talking about baking."

"We'll have to compare baking notes sometime." Mrs. O'Connell turned back to the kitchen.

Holly whispered, "I don't want this to be a lie. Reply to me with something about baking, please."

"Vanilla frosting is good on a chocolate cake?"

Holly stared at her in amazement. "You don't know how to bake, do you?"

"Does it count that I can lick the beaters? I have a friend who lets me do that sometimes."

Holly grinned. "It counts right now, but not in the real world."

Dropping her voice to a whisper again, Holly asked, "When is the joke being revealed?" She stopped for a moment and then raised an eyebrow, "Aren't you staying in his one-bedroom apartment?"

"No hanky-panky. I don't think he's actually interested in me in that way, anyway. I slept on the bed, and he slept on the sofa. But this morning, his parents, and his brothers Jack and Andy came by with a brand-new queen-size bed. And all the bedding. I'm unsure about what we're going to do if I stay another night because there are going to be questions about whether or not the bed was comfortable. I can see his mother asking that, can't you?"

Holly nodded.

"If things go according to Noah's plan, he's going to tell his mom, and everyone else, right after lunch and before dessert."

Holly narrowed her gaze. "Why do you say that with uncertainty?"

"Because thus far, it doesn't seem like anything about my trip to Alaska has gone according to plan."

At that moment, the men boisterously returned to the house.

His mother stepped out of the kitchen. "Lunch is ready. Everyone come on over. I have every extension in the table, so I think we can get everybody around it and be reasonably comfortable. A large dining area is one of the main reasons that we bought this house." She turned back toward the kitchen, then stopped and looked their way again. "I've always dreamed of my five boys sitting around my table with their wives. My dreams have come closer in this last year." With a smile, she turned back and went into the kitchen.

Rachel couldn't have felt any guiltier than she did right now.

They all did fit at the table and Noah was, of course, beside her. She put a scoop of mashed potatoes on her plate. "This all looks great, Mrs. O'Connell. Thank you for inviting us."

Noah's mother paused and said, "You're always welcome here, Rachel. You're now family."

Rachel felt tears stinging back of her eyes. These people had made her feel more welcome in the last day than her own family had in twenty-seven years. She smiled and took small portions of each of the dishes that were passed around the table. She'd barely be able to finish all of this. If the portions the men were piling on their plates were any indication, Mrs. O'Connell was used to preparing large amounts of food.

Jack asked, "Where are you planning to go for your honeymoon?" He looked right at Noah when he said it. Rachel glanced over at her "husband" and saw him glaring at his brother.

She stepped in. "I think our honeymoon is going to have to wait. Money right now is going into making sure that Noah's plane is safe to fly and in good shape."

Andy asked, "Will you need to find a job here in Kenai?"

That was one question they hadn't rehearsed. "I'm trying to sort that out right now. I've been part of the family business in Arlington, Virginia, all my life." She couldn't keep the melancholy note out of her voice. She sat with her hands on her lap, and Noah reached over and squeezed one. He always seemed to know when to do that to make her feel better. She'd miss that.

Mrs. O'Connell said, "I'm sure your family will feel the loss when you're here. Will they be able to run the business without you?"

"My parents have decided to sell the business because my brother wants to stay in Alaska. It's passed on from man to man." She used the ladle to put gravy on her mashed potatoes. The room grew quiet except for the two little girls talking at the other end of the table.

Noah's mother said, "You have no idea how odd that sounds to an Alaskan woman. I know I can do *anything*."

Rachel lifted the fork toward her mouth. "That's something I'm starting to appreciate, Mrs. O'Connell."

The closer they got to the end of the meal, the more Noah fidgeted beside her. He was planning to go through with the big reveal at the end. She was glad of that because these people were too nice to deceive. They had welcomed her in bizarre circumstances. She couldn't imagine most families welcoming a new bride when the couple had only known each other for a few days.

Noah leaned over and whispered in her ear, "During dessert." He looked her in the eye and nodded.

Okay, that took care of her appetite. This had just become too real. She got up to help clear the table after they'd eaten. When that was done, she and Jack brought back dessert plates and passed them around to everyone.

Mrs. O'Connell said from the kitchen, "This has been an exciting day. I'm so happy I can barely stand it."

When Rachel looked at Noah, he seemed stricken. This was going down much worse than he could have ever anticipated.

The front door opened, and a man with features much like the rest of the O'Connells but with brown hair like Andy walked in. "Can anyone join this party?"

"That's amazing," his mother said loudly from the kitchen. "That voice sounded exactly like Mark's. Did you call him and put him on speaker so he could be here?" She rounded the corner with a cake in her hands. When she saw the new man, she stopped, and her jaw dropped. Rachel jumped up and ran over. Surprise and the weight of a tall cake might not go well together.

When she reached her side, Mrs. O'Connell wobbled a little on her feet. Rachel took the cake from her hands as Mr. O'Connell and Adam hurried over.

"Mark? Are you really here?" With that, Noah's mother

crumpled, but the two men caught her before she hit the ground.

$$\sim$$

Mark rushed over to his mother. "Did she hit her head when she landed?"

Noah and the rest of his brothers hurried over too. Adam knelt next to his mother. "No, we caught her in time."

"Mom," Mark patted her cheek gently, "open your eyes."

Her eyes fluttered open, and she gazed up into Mark's face. "You're really here?"

"I'm not only here, Mom, I've got everything I own in that truck and trailer in front of your house."

She struggled to sit up. Once there, Mark supported her on one side and Noah on the other as she got to her feet. "I don't believe I have ever fainted in my entire life. I was so excited about Noah's marriage to this lovely girl Rachel that I thought I'd hallucinated you walking in the door." She gave him a friendly glare. "Because you never called to say you were on your way."

He smiled sadly. "Everyone else knew. It was supposed to be a happy surprise."

She hugged her son and pulled him tightly against her. "It's a happy moment. Don't you ever think that you walking in my door is anything but that."

Mark looked up at Noah, and his eyes widened. "I just realized that Mom said you're married! I must be really far out of the family loop because I didn't even know you'd found someone to date."

"Way to go, bro, making me sound like I'm completely inept at the dating scene."

Mark gave him a genuine smile. "You *have* been more focused on airplanes than women."

Noah chuckled. Rachel chose that moment to walk over and stand next to them.

Mark glanced around the room and then back at them. "Since she's the only woman I don't recognize, this must be your wife. Rachel, did Mom say?"

Mark had always had a great memory for details.

Rachel extended her hand to Mark. As he shook it, she said, "Noah and I met on Sunday."

Mark looked from one to the other. "Which Sunday?"

"The one that happened six days ago."

Noah watched his mother, and she seemed better now. Maybe he should confess. Jack came over and took him aside. "You can't tell her right now. I don't know if she's stable enough to take that. Mom normally rolls with whatever happens. She had to with five sons. But her fainting shows that we need to treat her gently for a while. I think you have to live with this for another day or two."

Noah knew his brother spoke the truth. But he was never one to lie. This simple joke wasn't supposed to last more than a day. On top of that, he now had to figure out where Rachel would spend the night.

His phone rang. As he took it out of his pocket to silence it and try to enjoy the rest of the meal with his family, he saw that it was from the airline's dispatcher. He hurried down the hall, away from all the noise and chaos, and answered the call.

"Noah?" his dispatcher's familiar voice asked.

"Yes. I'm here. Is something wrong?"

"We have a huge problem."

He hoped this wasn't about the move to Anchorage again.

He still hadn't been able to come to terms with being that far from his family, and he liked living in small-town Kenai. He thought about the mess he was in right now, though. He couldn't confess to his mom, and he couldn't live with Rachel in a one-bedroom apartment. He would not share the bed with her again, not outside of an emergency situation. And he could not bring himself to sleep on that sofa and really didn't want to keep sleeping on the floor.

"Colton's wife went into labor a month early. The baby's fine," she added quickly before he could ask, "but it's at the same time that Sarah is on vacation in Disney World. I know that she and her husband scrimped and saved for a year for the trip, so I don't want to ask her to come back and disappoint her kids. You're it, Noah."

He stared at the wall in front of him. "It? For what?"

"Everyone else is scheduled. We need you to fly out of Anchorage until Sarah's back from her vacation."

"Where would I live? I assume you want me to stay in Anchorage while I'm flying out of there."

"We do. Maybe you can get one of those temporary places that rents by the week. The airline can give you some money toward that, but we're still fairly small. It would also be helpful if you came to Anchorage today, so you could take a flight in the morning."

He didn't have a choice. He'd have to find a place to live tonight. He heard laughter from the other room and was glad that everything sounded normal again. "I'll be there. Text me everything I need to know."

He tucked the phone back into his pocket and headed out to the family. The expression on his face must have said that something had happened.

His dad asked, "Everything okay, son?"

Rachel was sitting next to his mother with an open photo album, no doubt with the expected embarrassing photos from his childhood. Judging from the sparkle in Rachel's eyes, it was definitely that.

Rachel's eyes sparkled as she looked at him and said, "Ribbit."

Oh yeah, Mom went all out with the embarrassing photos. He'd had a pet frog. They'd made him put it back in a pond. When he'd cried at losing his pet, his parents had bought him a stuffed animal frog which his mother had frequently reminded him as an adult was not easy to find. The photo no doubt showed him holding his live frog. Or it could be the one of him sleeping with his stuffed frog.

He glanced back at his father, who was still waiting for a reply. "I've been called to work in Anchorage because Colton is a father a full month early."

His mother looked up with concern in her eyes because she'd made a point of getting to know all of his coworkers and often brought treats for them to the office.

"Everyone's fine," Noah assured her. "But he's on leave." He shook his head and focused on the job ahead. All of the plans he needed to make for his move, the move he'd been avoiding, rushed in. "I need to pack my things and get to Anchorage on the next flight out, which leaves in an hour, so that I can find a place to live and be ready to fly out of there first thing in the morning."

His mother said in a steady voice, "Son, I believe you've forgotten something." Noah pulled himself out of his plans and focused on his mom. Then his eyes went to Rachel. Yes, he had forgotten something. He didn't need to find a one-bedroom place; he needed to find a two-bedroom home. Either that or one with an awesome sofa to sleep on. "Rachel, let's get out of here. We've got to get to the airport as soon as possible."

His oldest brother asked, "Wouldn't it be easier to drive? You won't have a vehicle in Anchorage if you don't."

Noah turned his wrist to check his watch. "Good point, Adam. We'll have less time today when we arrive, but having my truck would be better."

Rachel stood and walked over toward him. "Where are we going to live?" She looked him right in the eyes, signaling that he needed to be thinking of their separate living accommodations.

"I don't know. The airline is only giving us a small amount of money. I just don't know. It might be a studio apartment short-term in a not-great part of town."

Holly jumped to her feet. "I know!"

Everyone turned toward her.

"Adam, you remember that Bree and Michael are in New York for business for the next two weeks?" She explained to Rachel. "My brother-in-law's business was based in New York before he met Bree, my sister. When he moved the company headquarters to Anchorage, he left the New York office open, and they travel there fairly often."

"I've never been to their apartment in Anchorage." Noah said every word deliberately and slowly, wondering if living there could get them into more trouble instead of help. "Is it a one-bedroom?"

Holly laughed and stretched her hands wide. "Oh, it's much bigger than that. It's a three-bedroom condo with a view of the mountains that you wouldn't believe. Michael did very well with his software company."

Relief poured through Noah. "Are you sure they'll let us stay there?"

Holly waved his comment away. "Of course they will. You're family, and now Rachel is too." She smiled at Rachel. "I don't know about the dog, though. Adam and I can keep Zeke while you're staying at the condo. I can't say that he won't miss you, but . . ." She gestured to the two dogs they'd recently let back into the house. They must have been exhausted from playing because they were now sleeping side-by-side.

CHAPTER SIXTEEN

Rachel waited beside Noah when he called to let his dispatcher know he'd be driving to Anchorage instead of flying. They left about an hour later, heading out of Kenai on a highway that Rachel now recognized. She'd enjoyed Kenai. It was a nice town, but she was pretty sure she was not a small-town girl. She missed the activity and bustle of a city. Noah seemed to enjoy it, though.

"How long do you need to stay in Anchorage? I know you're based out of Kenai."

He sighed as he put on his signal to turn onto the highway. "It's a long story, Rachel."

She patted the dashboard. "I think we're going to be spending some quality time in this truck, so tell me the whole story."

He drove for a couple of minutes before he answered. "I like living in Kenai. I like having family nearby. I was in the Navy, and I didn't have any family nearby for years. At first, I saw that as a good thing because I got to be out on my own.

But after a while, I missed having everybody around. I missed Saturday lunch at my mom's."

"She does do quite a lunch."

He grinned and glanced over at her. "We look forward to it. If our schedules allow, we go."

"So you don't want to live in Anchorage?"

He steered around a car at the side of the road, where the owner was changing a tire. "I don't think I have a choice. They've repeatedly asked me to do it. And with Adam a short drive outside of Anchorage along with Holly and her girls, it feels a little like home."

"I guess you wouldn't want to leave the place where you grew up. Wait! I just remembered that this isn't your childhood home."

He laughed. "I grew up in the state capital, Juneau. My parents only moved here after we were out of high school. But we all love Kenai. Adam has a great position as a professor at the university in Anchorage, so he doesn't want to move anywhere else. But, as you can see, he and Holly come to Kenai fairly often."

"What I've seen of Anchorage made me think it was a small city. At least what I've seen of it from the airport and the car rental place."

"Anchorage is a little bit different than most places its size. It's the largest city in Alaska, but would be a medium-sized city in many other states. From there, it's a three-hour flight to Seattle, Washington, and the rest of the U.S. That means Anchorage has pretty much anything you can think of as far as businesses, medical care, and restaurants. And when you add on to that the fact that it's a major portal for tourists coming to Alaska—"

"I see now. It's a big little city."

"Yes. At least this move to Anchorage has solved the sleeping situation. From what Holly said, we'll have a great place."

They drove in silence for a few minutes. Rachel felt her eyelids getting droopy. "Noah, I keep thinking I've recovered from our adventure, but then I get sleepy. I'm going to take a nap if you don't need the company." They'd reached a pretty area with a sign that identified it as *Cooper Landing,* and it had a large river.

"If you weren't here, I would be driving or flying alone. I'm okay alone."

At her sharp intake of breath, he seemed to realize how his words could be interpreted. He quickly added, "But it's nice to have company."

She murmured, "It's nice to be here." And then she drifted off to sleep.

Rachel woke to a horn honking. They were on the outskirts of a city. "Noah, please don't tell me that I slept the entire drive."

"You did. And every once in a while, you snored."

"No, I didn't." She smacked his arm.

He glanced toward her and raised one eyebrow. Then he grinned. "No, you didn't. But you did drool a little bit." He pointed to his chin.

She swiped at her own chin, and her hand came back clean. Laughing, she said, "Stop it! I am sorry, though, that you had to drive in silence for hours. But the nap helped." The buildings grew closer together. "Are we almost downtown?"

"Not even close. Anchorage is pretty spread out. You could tell that from the air when we were coming in and going out."

"When we left, I didn't pay much attention because I thought it would never see it again beyond the airport, and I was focused on finding my brother. On the way back—" She stopped speaking as she realized she'd been so focused on Noah that she hadn't noticed the sights. "I wanted to get back to civilization." Quite true.

"As I said, Anchorage has almost anything you can imagine."

"I'm seeing that now as we drive. It doesn't seem like someone living here is lacking for much of anything."

"If you don't mind being a few days' drive to the Lower 48, then you have pretty much anything you would want." He pointed to their left. "Saltwater touches the city on that side, and mountains surround it."

Rachel looked around. She couldn't see water, but she could see mountains towering over them. "Have you ever climbed those mountains?"

"Remember, I didn't grow up here. But I have dreamed of climbing a few of the smaller ones when I fly in and out. It's somehow intriguing."

Downtown looked like what she guessed it would in many mid-size cities. Restaurants, hotels, and shops lined the street as they drove in. She even noticed one coffee shop not too far from the condo that might be a nice place to go while Noah was flying.

Before long, they were pulling into an underground parking garage at Michael and Bree's condo building in the middle of the city.

They stepped into the elevator. "Noah, when are you going to tell your family? My parents gave me ten days to come to Alaska and find David. I'm not sure any of that matters anymore, but I'd like to go back before that time is up."

The elevator doors opened, and they stepped out. Rachel waited while Noah opened the door to their unit. When she walked inside, the view through the windows pulled her forward. "Wow." She stood at the windows and stared at the mountains in the distance.

"That's apparently what sold Michael on this place." Noah stood beside her.

"Him? Not the couple?"

"He bought it before they were even officially dating. He hired Holly's oldest sister, Jemma, to decorate. And Bree came along. Of course, he and Bree had already met on a trip to the Alaska gold fields."

The hallway to her left seemed the only direction for the bedrooms, so she started that way. "Holly assured me that there is a master bedroom and a guest bedroom. She also told me that Bree is pregnant, and that she and Michael are buying things for the nursery in New York. We're fortunate to be here now and not in a month or two when they've converted their guest room to a nursery."

"Hold it. Holly knows about us? She must have, or she wouldn't have told you there was anything more than the so-important master bedroom for the newly married couple."

Rachel turned around. "She guessed, Noah. Your brothers, other than Jack, seemed to have bought into the whole thing. Holly knew something wasn't right. We chatted while you were out in the workshop with your dad."

He nodded. "I'm not surprised. What surprises me is the length of time this thing has held together. I will probably never play a practical joke on anyone again for the rest of my life."

The boisterous group of men that were his brothers and father, along with his mother who had started all of this, made Rachel fairly sure that was not true. "I don't think you can escape being part of another practical joke. Once this is revealed..."

He groaned. "They'll all want to get back at me. I never considered that. Let's check out these rooms." He entered the first door on the left. A big bed faced the windows, and frames with photos of a couple at a wedding decorated a dresser. "This is the master bedroom. Let's continue down the hall."

They found an office next. It had three monitors set up on a desk. Very geek-ready. The next door opened to a half bath and then there was a guest room. She stepped inside. "This is beautiful. Feminine but not over-the-top. If I lived in Anchorage, I would certainly have . . . what did you say the oldest sister's name was?"

"Jemma."

"I would have Jemma decorate my home. I'm happy to take this room, Noah, if you'd like the master." She opened a door and found an attached bath. When she turned around, she ran into him. "I'm sorry. I didn't realize you'd followed me in here."

Noah put a hand on each of her shoulders to steady her. When she looked up into his eyes, they both froze. He brushed her hair away from her face.

She so much wanted to kiss this man. Rachel rose on her tiptoes and held his gaze as she moved closer. When her lips were an inch away from his, she hesitated.

Noah crushed her to him, kissing her deeply. He pulled away and kissed down the side of her neck before coming back to her mouth. She wrapped her arms around him and pulled him close, drinking in the kiss.

When he stepped back, Rachel put her hand on her mouth. His expression switched from happiness to regret.

She expected him to say something, maybe not words of love but at least of interest. Instead, he said, "I'm sorry, Rachel. I shouldn't have done that." He turned and left the room.

Rachel had no more doubts that this man was interested in her. At least physically. But maybe nothing more. As she stood there, a soft bump on her ankle startled her. A cat sat and stared up at her. No one had mentioned this resident of the condo.

She knelt to pet the cat. His collar said, *Stitches*. "At least I know you like me, Stitches. Or is it that you want to be fed?"

The cat began purring and bumped her hand. "I wish men could be this obvious about affection." Rachel sighed.

A short time later, Holly sent a text that said, *There's a cat. Stitches. Feeding directions on the fridge.* A few seconds later, another text arrived that said, *I hope you like cats.*

Rachel and Noah went to dinner in a somewhat noisy, nearby restaurant, one that Noah knew about. The volume made it difficult to talk, and about halfway through the meal, Rachel began to wonder if that's why he had chosen it. Things were noticeably awkward between them since the kiss.

When they arrived back at the condo, Noah gave her a long glance before saying, "I have an early flight, so I don't think I'll see you in the morning. But I'll be home for dinner tomorrow." He handed her the key. "I assume you'll be here."

Was he asking her if she would be in the state of Alaska or in the condo? "I'll be here." She held his gaze for a moment, then he went down the hall to the master bedroom, and she heard the door close.

Plans. She needed plans for her life. The situation with Noah was extremely temporary. He could end it by sending a text message to his father, something like, *Dad, I'm sorry it was all a joke. Please break it to Mom gently.* Only she knew he wouldn't do that because the man she knew had more honor than that. He would want to tell his mother himself.

So that left her in a condo in the middle of the night in Anchorage, Alaska, with a man down the hall who ran hot and cold with interest in her.

Against her better judgment, she became more and more interested in him every day. That meant she either needed to spend less time with him while she was here or head back to her empty existence in Virginia. Soon. A third choice came to mind as she was about to fall asleep. She could enjoy the moment with Noah and whatever romance happened in their few days left together. It might help fill some of the emptiness later.

CHAPTER SEVENTEEN

*N*oah leaned against the bedroom's closed door. What had he been thinking when he kissed Rachel? He straightened and walked across the room to the window. Daylight was fading, but he could still see the mountains in the distance. Those mountains felt solid, like everything that was in his path right now.

Should he move to Anchorage or not? Was there a good way out of this practical joke? Whether there was or not, he had to find a way to get Rachel as far away from him as he could.

He liked her.

He turned and walked toward the bathroom to get ready for bed. No, he more than liked her. He'd been her protector in Petersville. She'd quickly shown him she could take care of herself after that and stepped in to take care of him when he needed it. It reminded him of his parents' relationship.

He picked up his toothbrush and put toothpaste on it. Then he stared into the mirror. Rachel's life pulled her away from Alaska. She'd made it clear that her talents and services were needed on the East Coast. He pushed aside any thoughts of interest beyond friendship and got to work brushing his teeth.

Tomorrow. Tomorrow he'd find a way to reveal the joke. He hoped someone was laughing when he did that. Then Rachel would be on the next flight out of here, he'd never see her again, and life would go back to the way it had been. He'd be happy by himself. He'd keep telling himself right up to that moment. He hoped he was right.

The next morning, Noah quietly opened the bedroom door, peered out into the hallway, and softly walked down the hall to the kitchen where he scrounged in the cupboards and found some healthy snack bars. He snagged one, making a mental note that he would need to buy some to replace it before they left. He didn't bother with coffee because he figured that would make too much noise, and he really didn't want to face Rachel this morning. *Wrap it up, O'Connell. Move on.* He exited the condo. The second the door closed, he knew he'd left his flight bag inside.

He rested his forehead against the door, then straightened and pushed the doorbell.

Rachel opened the door a few minutes later, her hair messy and her eyes sleepy. And she'd never been more beautiful.

"I need to get my flight bag. I forgot it." He pointed around her.

She pulled the door open wider. He stepped in, snagged it, and turned around.

"Dinner, right?" She looked up at him with an expression that said she remembered last night's kiss. The kiss he'd been doing his best to forget.

"I think so." He hurried toward the elevator, knowing she

must have expected a goodbye kiss after last night. That would never happen again.

~

Rachel decided that since she was up, she was up. There was no point going back to bed. She thought about putting on a pot of coffee, then decided it might be best to go a local coffee shop, that one they'd driven by on the way in, and let them make coffee for her. They probably had something to eat there too.

A glance at the clock on the stove told her that the time difference would make this a decent time to call her parents, not ideal but okay. Maybe they'd had time to process their thoughts about her brother. Or maybe the sale had fallen through, and they would finally consider letting her run the business.

Fortified with a hot shower and with the remaining sleep washed away, Rachel picked up her phone and stared at it. This single call would define her future. Either they'd changed their mind, or she would be on her own to make a new career and a new life. She just didn't know what that meant yet.

She hit *call* and two rings later her mother answered the phone.

"Are you on your way back?"

How to phrase this so she didn't sound frivolous? Her parents always accused her of not being businesslike, and yet she had been with every fiber of her being and with every action. "I stayed behind in Alaska to wrap things up. I should be home in a couple of days."

Rachel heard her dad's deep voice in the background, but

couldn't make out the words. "Your father says he's disappointed that you aren't here now."

Happiness raced through her. Her father wanted her?

"The transfer of ownership will go more smoothly if we have extra help." Her mother's words stilled any happiness. She wasn't wanted for herself but for her help.

"You have definitely decided to sell the business? What will happen to Fitzpatrick's?"

Her dad's gravelly tones came over the phone. "A man with three sons is buying the business. It will go on. The contract is signed. We simply need to wrap up our portion of it." He must have passed the phone back to her mother because it was her voice that said, "We'll expect you in the office in two days." Rachel pulled her phone away from her ear and watched as the call ended from the other end, feeling her hopes die with it.

The peaceful mountains outside the windows beckoned to her, so she wandered over to take that in. She didn't have many friends at home anymore, at least not close friends. The people she had known in high school were almost all married with children and living their own lives. Those she went to college with were scattered around the globe. Friendships needed care, and she hadn't given them that care.

She focused on the next steps in front of her. Wrap this up today with Noah and his family. Catch a flight tomorrow. Be at work on Wednesday.

A bird flew by, and she admired its freedom. *You don't know what that means until you realize you don't have it.*

A soft bump against her leg startled her. Stitches looked up at her like he was saying, *Where's my breakfast, and could you pet me, please?* She sat down on the floor to pet him. Then she got up and fixed the food per the directions that Bree had left on the front of the fridge.

A quick text to Holly had gotten her the answer that she'd hoped for: Michael gave her permission to use the laptop sitting in his office. A half-hour later, she walked into the Kobuk, a cute gift shop with a coffee shop and café at the back. She set the laptop she'd brought on a table near a window and walked up to order, choosing their apparently popular samovar tea instead of coffee and an Alaska birch syrup glazed old fashioned doughnut. She sat down at the table and fired up the computer. It had a bunch of apps on it that she'd had never heard of, but fortunately, it also had a word processing program she knew well.

A minute later, a blank screen stared at her, and the cursor flashed as if to say *Put something useful here.*

She typed, *What do I do with my life?*

Her tea arrived. As she took a sip of the delicious beverage and then ate a bite of a doughnut she would probably never forget for the rest of her life because it was so amazing, words came to her and she typed them.

What would you like to do, Rachel?

Never in her entire life had she gotten to have the freedom to choose. No, that wasn't true. In her off hours, she chose what her heart enjoyed most. She typed that.

Fashion.

What could she do with that? Should she get a job in women's fashion? Would that be in a retail store either large or small? Should she work in fashion design in New York City?

She thought about what else she enjoyed. If she were starting over, it might as well be something she loved. She added that to the page.

Sales.

When she'd been allowed to step out from behind a desk —no, not really allowed, but when she was needed in the store during the holidays or when someone else was out— she'd enjoyed the one-on-one contact with customers. So it wasn't only sales, because you could do that online, it was being able to talk to people. After backspacing over *Sales*, she typed her new version.

One-on-one sales.

She considered the other aspects of the work that she had been doing for so many years. Did she like any of it? The cursor continued to flash. She went through her daily and weekly routine. She didn't *dislike* her job and the tasks it included so much as she didn't *enjoy* it. She could competently balance a spreadsheet, but she knew deep in her heart that wasn't what she wanted to do every day in another job.

Design.

As she typed that word, her heart sang. She had a closet filled with her designs, clothing that had never seen the light of day. Some of it in her size, but some petite and some curvy so that she could test her skills and see what worked best in different sizes of clothing. To play with patterns and styles.

Rachel checked her list. *Fashion. One-on-one sales. Design.* She leaned back and looked around the unique and friendly shop she was in. It didn't have a cookie-cutter chain feel, and she liked that. It was probably family-owned. Could she also have her own business? A kernel of an idea grew in her heart.

What if she had a clothing store?

The idea grew and grew. Like the bird she'd seen outside of the windows, it gave her a sense of freedom as it danced in her heart. She began typing as the ideas flew into her mind. She would have a store. She would carry clothing she designed and other clothing, too, in all sizes. The pretty and casual design style she'd honed for years would be welcomed by women. It was young and fun, but she thought it would appeal to women of all ages. The store would be girly but not old-fashioned.

Living cheaply, simply because she had little time for vacations and entertainment, would pay off. Sure, she spent some money on fashion, but her one-bedroom condo had definitely been under budget.

She popped the last bite of the doughnut in her mouth and finished her tea. Then, laptop tucked under her arm, she decided to walk and explore while her new life became clearer and clearer in her mind. The area nearby had a convention center, hotels, and restaurants. She suspected this was a part of the city that tourists would frequent.

The vision for her business became so clear that when she saw an empty storefront with a 'for lease' sign in the window, she could picture her shop there. Tourists would probably like her clothing style. They'd be able to wear most of the clothes on their trip and also after they returned home.

She could see her sign out front. She envisioned the room she saw through the window filled with clothes, her standing there with a customer, and maybe an assistant ready to help other customers. It felt successful. And she knew she could do this. A little twinge of doubt crept in, but she pushed it away. No, she had all the skills to do this. And more.

After snapping a photo, so she could keep the vision for her store clear in her mind, she turned away and continued her walk. Now she needed to find a place like that near her home in Virginia.

Rachel opened the door and danced into the condo, thrilled to be able to tell Noah about her new plans tonight.

A woman stared at her from the kitchen. Rachel shrieked and stepped back.

They both said, "Who are you?" at the same time.

Rachel looked around the condo to make sure it was the right one. Yes. Besides, the key had fit in the lock, so it had to be the right one. "I'm supposed to be here."

"So am I. I'm Michael's mother. Please tell me you aren't his little bit on the side."

Rachel laughed. "I'm no one's little bit on the side. I'm here with Noah O'Connell."

"Adam's brother." The woman nodded. "Bree said Adam's brother would be staying for a few days. I didn't realize he was married." She frowned. "In fact, I'm surprised I wasn't invited to the wedding. We're always invited to the larger family events."

Rachel felt her face grow hot. How did she explain her situation to a stranger? She could barely explain it to herself. "It's a long story." Did she dare hope that Michael's mother was on her way to an appointment and needed to leave?

The woman started walking toward a sofa in the living room. "I'm Patricia Kinkaid. I have a feeling it's an interesting story, and I have all the time we need."

Seated across from Mrs. Kinkaid, Rachel found herself once again explaining how she and Noah met and the situation she now found herself in. When she got the end to the end of the tale, or at least brought it to this moment—the end remained uncertain—Mrs. Kinkaid said, "Rachel, I have never heard a story like this in my life. It's worthy of television. It actually might make a great movie by that channel that makes all those wholesome movies." She leaned forward. "It *is* wholesome, right? You didn't leave out any . . . interesting parts?"

Rachel felt a blush come over her face. Once again, her fair skin would reveal all. "I'm in the guest room, and he's in the master."

Mrs. Kinkaid processed that for a second before speaking. "So there's no hanky-panky going on?"

Were a few kisses hanky-panky? Could they fit into that category? It might not hurt to have the advice of somebody older and wiser. She couldn't go to her mother, and she certainly couldn't ask Noah's mother. This woman seemed to be someone who would tell her exactly what she thought, and Rachel so appreciated that.

She cleared her throat. "Only if three kisses count." Rachel felt her skin grow even hotter.

Mrs. Kinkaid gave her a scrutinizing stare. "I wouldn't call that going too far for the situation, but I don't think you would have kissed a man you weren't interested in having more of a relationship with. Am I right?"

Mrs. Kinkaid's eyes seemed to bore straight through her and into her soul. She must have been a formidable mother during her children's teen years. As Rachel formulated an answer, the older woman watched her without saying anything or moving a muscle. It was almost eerie.

"I'll tell you the truth—"

The woman gave a single nod.

"When we were lost in Petersville and Noah kissed me, it was comforting in a sweet way." Rachel considered how to describe last night's kiss. The emotions she'd felt at that moment rushed back into her. "Last night felt like so much more. I felt like I wanted to hold on to Noah forever." She opened her eyes with a sigh.

"I'm not going to put myself in the role of describing your emotions and how your heart feels, Rachel." Mrs. Kinkaid looked sympathetic. "But I will ask, are you in love with Noah O'Connell?"

Rachel rolled her eyes. "How can you love someone you've known for one week?"

Mrs. Kinkaid raised her eyebrows. "We've all heard about love at first sight."

She thought of her conversation with Holly about that very subject. "Mrs. Kinkaid, I'm not sure that I even know what love feels like. Do I care for Noah? Sure. Do I enjoy spending time with him? Absolutely. Will I miss him when I leave here? Once again a yes. But is that love, or is it friendship?"

Mrs. Kinkaid stood. "Only you have the answer to that, Rachel. If you feel a bond with him like no other? If you smile just because you're in the same room with him? If you look forward to the next time you'll see him, and if his holding your hand makes your heart sing? You may have found love. The calendar can't tell you whether it's love or not. Love can come in a second, or it can take years.

"My daughter Leah met Ben and decided to marry him within days. They seem very happy." She patted Rachel on the arm and headed for the door, leaving Rachel with more questions than answers.

The door closed with a thump. Rachel blinked then looked around the now empty condo. She would have thought she'd met an angel if it wasn't for the fact that there was a bowl of cat food sitting where none had been earlier.

CHAPTER EIGHTEEN

*N*oah flew three back-and-forth flights from Anchorage to the Kenai Peninsula. The last one, in the early afternoon, took him to Kenai. As the plane taxied up to the terminal so the passengers could disembark, he knew he needed to get over to his parents to explain his *marriage*. He shouldn't put it off any longer.

He checked the time. The return flight wouldn't be for about ninety minutes, so he had about an hour, and his parents lived ten minutes or less from the airport. He could do this. He'd wanted Rachel to be there, but maybe it was best she wasn't, in case it didn't go over well.

He let the dispatcher know he would be in Kenai and returning in time for his flight, then hurried out to the front of the terminal to catch one of the taxis lined up and waiting for passengers.

Minutes later, he stood on his parents' front step with his hand raised to knock. He'd never been a chicken. He rapped on the door, and a minute later, his mother opened it.

"Noah! This is a pleasant surprise." She leaned to the side to look around him. "Rachel isn't with you?"

He stepped inside and followed her over to the living room. "No. I'm flying today, and I have a break in-between flights. Rachel's in Anchorage."

"I hope she's not lonely there. She seems like such a nice girl, the woman you chose for your wife." She sat on the sofa. "I do wish, of course, that you had known her longer before you married her, but I'm happy to welcome her into the family."

His father chose that moment to walk in the back door. "I worked through lunch again, anything I can just grab?" He stepped into the living area, saw his son, and came over. "Everything okay, Noah?"

Noah sighed. He may as well get this over with now. Chatting for a while first wasn't going to make it any easier. "If you could sit down for a minute, Dad, I have something I'd like to tell you and Mom." The older man hesitated for a moment then came over and sat down with a worried expression.

"Is—"

"Everyone's okay. This isn't about anyone's health or safety."

Both of his parents relaxed.

"But it is about my marriage." He used air quotes around the word.

Just say it, Noah, he said to himself. "We are not married."

"What?!" His mother rose to her feet and glared at him.

His father reached up and patted his wife's arm. "Let him speak, honey. I think he has something he needs to tell us."

She gave him another glare but sat back on the sofa with her arms crossed.

"There isn't anything going on between us, Mom. Do you remember when you talked her into speaking with an Irish accent to trick me?"

A glimmer of a smile hovered around his mother's mouth. "Of course I do. And that brought the two of you together." Now she had the satisfied smile of a successful matchmaker. He hated to wipe that off her face.

"I had this genius idea of paying you back. Rachel didn't just take a forty-five-minute flight with me, she had to spend two days in the wilderness with me, walking out of a dangerous situation through roaring rivers, skirting areas with bears and more. I thought what if . . .?"

A sparkle lit his mother's eyes. She had an inkling of what was about to be said.

His father chuckled. "You decided to pretend you were married so that your mother didn't have the thrill of planning a wedding." His father nodded. "That is a genius idea, Noah. It kind of blew up all around you, though, didn't it?"

Noah groaned. "You bought us the bed. She'd slept on my twin bed that night, and I slept on the floor in the living room. We'd already had to camp out for two nights, so that was not a big deal."

His mother had a frosty tone to her voice when she asked, "And now? What about last night?"

"Bree and Michael have an amazing condo with a view of the mountains that you wouldn't believe and three bedrooms. I slept in the master, and Rachel slept in the guest room. She got the cat as a sleeping companion. He seems to like her better than me."

Her mother laughed. "Why did you let this joke ride so long, son?"

"You fainted, Mom. You were so overjoyed about me, and

then Mark walked in the room, and you fainted. I was opening my mouth to reveal all."

His mother's eyes widened. "So not only did you *not* marry her, you don't have any relationship with her, do you? She won't be part of our family?"

"No, Mom. I'm sorry. She has to go home to Virginia."

His mother looked sad, and he wished he hadn't caused that. "I am surprised. You seemed to genuinely care for each other. I thought you'd found your match."

Noah stood. "Only because you wanted to be the matchmaker. I need to get back to the airport. Dad, could you drive me? I took a taxi over here, but I didn't make him wait."

"Sure, son." His father got up, and the two of them walked over to the door. Noah glanced over his shoulder and saw his mother with that same sad expression. So much for a great practical joke.

Maybe the joke was on him. He'd ended up finding a woman that he might have been able to see a future with, but his future was here and hers was somewhere else. The two men drove in silence. When he pulled up to drop Noah off, his father said, "Rachel seems like someone you care deeply for. I don't usually say things like that, but I want you to consider everything you're doing with her very carefully."

Noah patted his dad on the arm, got out of the truck, and went into the airport to take the flight back to Anchorage and Rachel.

How would she take the news that there was no need for them to be together any longer?

~

Was she in love with Noah? Rachel mulled that thought over in her mind. Could that be true? She said the words out loud to test them. "I love Noah."

Thinking about him brought a song to her heart and a smile to her face. It had happened quickly, beyond anything she could have even anticipated. She did love Noah. Maybe that was the magic of Alaska. It wasn't love at first sight, but one week didn't seem much different. Not to her logical mind, anyway, which had always gone by the rules. The rule in her mind said you knew someone for a while, you dated him, it became more serious, and then you fell in love. But her heart wasn't playing by the rules.

A knock on the door brought her out of her thoughts. She went over to answer it and smiled broadly when she saw Noah through the peephole. She opened the door, and before he had even stepped through it, she put her arms around him and pulled him close. "I'm so glad to see you again."

He stilled. If he had a twin, she would have wondered if that's who this was. She released him and stepped back. What had happened after last night's kiss to change him so much? He'd been a bit cooler toward her after that, but this was glacial.

He stepped around her and into the room. "I'm sorry, Rachel, it's been a very long day. I'm also sorry you had to spend it alone."

"I met Michael's mother. She lives in the same building and came up to feed the cat." Something had happened to Noah while he'd been gone.

"Are you okay, Noah?"

He looked down at himself and then up at her. "I'm fine. What if I change out of my uniform, and we go to dinner?"

This time she did smile. Maybe everything was okay, but he'd had a long day. That could happen to anyone.

He went down the hall and disappeared through the door to the master bedroom. Five minutes later, he came out wearing dress pants and a dress shirt. "Ready?"

She nodded. Then he held her hand, and they went out the door. They found a nice restaurant a block away and were quickly seated because it was still early in the evening. As soon as the waiter had brought their water and left, they both leaned forward and spoke at the same time.

She said, "I have great news."

Noah said, "I have to tell you what happened today."

"You first." Noah pointed at Rachel, who took a sip of her water.

"I went over to that cute little coffee shop and gift store not far from the condo and planned my life."

Noah buttered a slice of bread and took a bite before speaking. After swallowing, he said, "Your whole life?"

She laughed. "Well, maybe not my whole life. But my work life. I realized that I wanted to have my own clothing store. Remember how I told you about the fashions that I've sewn? And the many that I've designed?"

"Yes, believe it or not, I remember all of those details. I even remember that you made a friend's wedding dress."

It was a good man who remembered things that had so little importance to him but were important to her. "Well, I realized that I enjoy one-on-one time with customers and that I know a lot about retail and like it. I've decided to open my own clothing store."

"Have you given up on the idea that your parents won't sell?"

She'd forgotten that she hadn't talked to Noah since she'd

made the last call home. It didn't even feel like home anymore. "I talked to them this morning. They'd *already* sold it, and the contract has been signed. They need me back in the office by Wednesday so I can help with the transfer."

Noah's face dropped when she said *Wednesday*.

She brought out her phone and showed him the photo she'd snapped of the building. "This is about the right size, and it seems to be a good location for what I want to do." She told him where it was.

"I don't know as much about Anchorage as someone like Adam or Michael would, but I think that anything near here would be a good place." Excitement lit his face. "Did you call them to find out about leasing?"

This was not her home. She was a city girl through and through, and she belonged in Georgetown or Arlington or somewhere nearby. "Noah, this is an example of what I want. But I need to find that in Virginia. Hopefully somewhere near my condo." She softly said the words and put her hand over his.

He stared at her with sad eyes. "My news will wrap this up then." He hesitated for a moment before speaking. "When I was in Kenai between flights, I went over and told Mom and Dad about the joke."

Rachel set down her glass of water with a stunned expression. "So it's all over?"

"We don't need to be together anymore," Noah said. The words cut straight through her heart. "You're free to go. Make a great life for yourself, Rachel." He slipped his hand out from under hers and sat back in his chair.

Their dinners arrived, but Rachel knew she couldn't eat a bite. She rose to her feet. "Then I guess this is goodbye." She reached over and put her hand on Noah's cheek for a moment. Then she walked out of the restaurant and into the evening, her eyes blurry with tears that she blinked to hold in. She walked faster and faster as she got closer to her temporary home.

Inside the condo, she threw herself down on the sofa and let out a wail. It was over. Her time here had all been like a mist. It was there, and now it was gone. She wiped her tears. Noah could be back any minute. After taking out her phone, she searched for flights. It seemed there were many of them that left very late at night or early in the morning. She chose one with good connections to Washington D.C., bought it with the Fitzpatrick's company credit card, and got up to put her things into her suitcase. She'd leave now so she didn't have to face Noah again. She had a feeling he was going to come back here as soon as he paid the bill. At least that's what she would have done.

With everything loaded, she gave Stitches a final pet and left. In the elevator, she realized she had the key, and Noah would have no way to get in, so she hit the button for the floor Michael's mother lived on. She knocked on the door and was grateful to find her at home.

"Would you please give Noah this key when he comes home? I'm going to text him to let him know you have it." She forced a smile, hoping the other woman didn't ask any questions, full well knowing that was a slim chance.

"Broke up with him, hmmm?" Mrs. Kinkaid raised her eyebrows at Rachel.

Rachel wet her lips. "Yes, ma'am. I'm on my way to the airport now."

"Love isn't always as we think it is. It can survive things we wouldn't expect it to survive, and it can be shattered by things that seem simple. If you have true love, Rachel, hold on to it."

Rachel thanked her and headed for the elevator. The car she'd called was waiting for her out front, and she was soon on her way to the airport, wondering if she would ever hear from or see Noah O'Connell again. She guessed not, unless they happened to see each other when she came to Alaska to visit David, Katie, and the baby.

As the plane took off and rose higher in the sky, taking her away from Anchorage, Rachel realized that not only had Noah stolen her heart, Alaska had taken a piece of it too. It was wild and unexpected and dangerous at times, but it was also unique and friendly and the place that Noah called home.

She picked up a fashion magazine she'd bought at the airport, but it was hard to concentrate on it. The upcoming changes in her life kept pulling her attention away. She had to help wrap up her parents' business. Then she could spend one hundred percent of her time on her own business.

She'd find the perfect location for it and make a life so filled with activity that she wouldn't think about Alaska or Noah.

CHAPTER NINETEEN

*N*oah went into the apartment he'd rented in Anchorage right after Rachel left and dropped his flight bag by the door. He'd spent the morning with a run up to Fairbanks and had thought about Rachel when his route home had brought him near Talkeetna and Petersville.

Of course, he'd thought about her every day since she'd left. Little things reminded him of her. He'd started using a different mug for his coffee just so he wouldn't picture the cute smirk on her face when she handed him the other mug.

He sat down on his sofa in his small living room, leaned back, and tried to get comfortable. Someday he'd go shopping for less tortuous furniture. Zeke jumped on the sofa next to him, and Noah absently scratched behind his ears.

A knock sounded on his door. Expecting it to be the pizza he'd ordered on his way home, he hurried over to the door, hoping he'd worked up an appetite to eat it. Another knock came before he got there. The pizza delivery person might find their tip shrinking if they knocked one more time before he could get across the small room.

When he opened the door, he found no pizza but instead his four brothers packed together in the hallway.

Adam came in first, and the others filed in behind him.

"Nothing's happened to Mom or Dad, right?" he asked quickly.

Adam kept going, leading the pack. "No. We're here for a brotherly intervention." At Adam's voice, Zeke jumped down to see what was going on.

Adam took the living room chair, and the other three men crowded onto the small sofa, leaving Noah to drag over a chair from his dining table, Zeke trailing behind.

Noah spun the chair around and sat facing the back, wondering how bad this was going to be.

They all looked to Adam to lead the discussion. "We're concerned about you, Noah," he said bluntly.

Noah stared at his older brother. "Why?"

Jack said, "You've lost weight. You aren't eating well and taking good care of yourself."

"Not true. I have pizza on the way."

Adam continued the conversation. "Noah, every time we come over here, there's a pizza box on the counter. Is that all you're eating?"

Noah thought about it. The last month did seem kind of jumbled. He only ate when he felt hungry, but he did make sure he had food every night. "I had Mexican one day last week." There, take that.

"And what about this place?" Mark asked.

Noah looked around the small room which was his living room, kitchen, and dining area all in one. "What about it? I had to get an apartment here in Anchorage."

Adam sighed and leaned forward in his chair, resting his elbows on his thighs and his chin on his fists. "This is in the worst part of town. Did you not pay attention to where you were? This is a safe city for the most part, but every city has an area most people would not choose to live in. You chose it."

Noah pictured the streets leading to his apartment and the general appearance of it. A few boards were coming off the exterior, and the building needed to be painted. Used furniture had been left at the curb a couple weeks ago. Someone must have moved and not wanted it anymore. Could his brothers be right?

He rubbed his temples. "I needed an apartment. I came to the cheapest one I saw and rented it. I like it here." Or at least, he didn't *dislike* it here.

At that moment, someone's music kicked up high. He'd normally ignore it. Someone shouted at someone else in the parking lot. Noah did his best to smile and pretend that everything was okay.

Andy stared at him. "Noah, you're wandering through life right now."

Noah rested his forehead on the back of the chair. "I don't know how I got here. I had an apartment in Kenai that I liked. Then I was at Bree and Michael's. It feels like one day I woke up and I was here."

The argument in the parking lot escalated, turning into a shouting match. Then a car door slammed, and tires squealed as it pulled out of the parking lot.

Adam asked in a gentle, big-brother voice, "Have you called her?"

Emotions rushed into Noah. He pushed them away. It was over. He swallowed hard. "I won't even pretend that I don't know who you're talking about. Rachel left to return to a life she likes in Virginia. She was only here to find her brother."

"I'm probably not the best one to talk about resolving your past, but are you sure that's what she wants?" Mark asked.

Noah lifted his head and looked at Mark, a man who'd also had a painful dating experience. Again, Noah thought back over his last conversation with Rachel, as he had hundreds of times, often in the middle of the night when all he could think about was her. Her blue eyes smiling at him. Her gorgeous red hair glinting in the sun.

One of his brothers cleared his throat, pulling Noah out of his thoughts. He squinted for a second, remembering that Mark had asked a question. What was it? Oh, right, whether Rachel really wanted her life in Virginia.

"I don't know. Not anymore. I thought I did. I was so sure. I know she had to go back to help with her family business and that she likes cities."

Jack said, "Now we're getting somewhere. Did she say anything positive about Anchorage? I know it's not a city on the scale of the ones she's used to, but it has a lot to offer. If you like cities. Which I don't."

Those words made Noah grin for the first time in a very long time. "Thanks, bro." Their last dinner together played in his mind. "She realized she wanted to open a women's clothing store. She showed me a photo of a place downtown that was available and would be perfect for her shop."

Andy said, "Well, then—"

"But she followed that up by saying she had to find a place like it near her condo in Virginia."

All four of his brothers sank back in their seats, and silence fell over the room.

Adam picked the conversation back up a minute later. "We all agree you should try contacting her. What if she misses Alaska and maybe even a scroungy mutt of a brother named Noah?"

Did he dare hope? A knock sounded on his door, and Noah stood to answer it. "I'm sorry, guys, but I only ordered pizza for one."

Adam laughed. "We were pretty certain you would order pizza tonight, so we went ahead and called your usual pizzeria to add to your order."

Noah opened the door and found the pizza delivery guy with a stack of four pizzas, plates, and napkins. Jack had followed him to the door where he paid the delivery guy while Noah carried the boxes over to the table.

As they all crowded around his thrift store table to get their food, Noah knew this was what he'd been missing, this time with his family. He had withdrawn and hadn't even noticed it. He hadn't been to a Saturday lunch for weeks.

With plates loaded high with several pieces of pizza each, Andy grabbed one of the dining room chairs and started dragging it toward the living room with one hand while he balanced his plate of pizza in the other.

Jack said, "Good idea." Then he also grabbed one of the chairs and so did Mark.

Sitting on his chair, Mark agreed. "That is the worst sofa I've sat on in my life. I think boards would be more comfortable."

"I second that," Jack said.

Laughing, Noah sat on his chair. "It is awful, isn't it? Notice how it coordinates with the gray theme that was in my other apartment." He realized that this apartment didn't have a theme beyond shabby, with stained carpet and walls that needed to be repainted.

Adam said, "Mom?"

Noah nodded as he took a bite of his pizza. "She decorated the day I signed the lease on my Kenai apartment. I'm actually surprised she hasn't been over here to do that."

Adam and Mark looked at each other.

Mark said, "We told her not to come, Noah. It isn't the best part of town."

Noah munched on his pizza as he thought about what they'd said. A baby crying from the apartment below startled him. At least that was a normal sound. But in most places, it wouldn't feel as though he was sharing the room with the baby. "I may need to find another place. My job here has become permanent, at least for a while, so I'm staying in Anchorage."

The brothers looked at each other again, and then Adam shook his head.

Noah wondered what that was all about, but knowing Adam, he'd find out when his older brother decided he was ready to share.

When they'd all finished eating, Noah got out a trash bag for the plates and started for the fridge with the leftovers.

Adam put his hand on Noah's shoulder. "Don't bother with that. We can take those with us. There's one more thing I wanted to talk about." He gestured with his head back to the seating area.

A door slammed somewhere down the hall and Noah winced.

When they were seated, Adam resumed the conversation. "As I said, when we arrived, we're staging an intervention here. As I understand it—and before you say anything, yes, I did contact the landlord to see what your terms were—you're paying by the month, and you don't have a lease. Correct?"

Noah felt a little annoyed that his family was checking up on him to this extent, but he answered, "Correct."

"Then you're out of here tonight."

Noah was about to argue that he was fine here, but shouting began down the hall, and flashing lights outside grew brighter. When he went over to the window, a police car pulled up to the building, two officers got out, and hurried inside.

How had he managed to choose what must be the worst place in a city of hundreds of thousands of people?

He turned away from the window. His brothers all had no-nonsense expressions on their faces. "It's possible that I may not have chosen my apartment wisely. I will find a new location soon."

His mind had trouble wrapping around the situation he now realized he was in.

Adam stood. "We've got you covered, bro. And before you argue, know that we'd expect you to do this for any one of us if we are ever in a situation like this. I don't care how old we are or how far away we might be. Got that?"

Noah nodded slowly. What was about to happen?

Adam said, "Let's get going, guys!"

His brothers all stood, grabbed the chairs they were sitting on, and started for the door, which Adam propped open.

"Hey? What are you doing?"

"We have a moving van outside. We rented it for the evening along with a storage unit to put your things in until you find something better. You're spending the night with me. We'll talk about your future tomorrow. Are you good with that?" His older brother's sentence had a question mark at the end, but it didn't really feel like one. His family was here to help him, and he needed to go along with it. He'd figure out his next steps tomorrow.

When his brothers returned and started for the sofa, he stopped them. "Leave that. Maybe the next renter will like it more than I do."

Andy grinned. "Good choice. And next time when you're ready to choose a sofa—"

"I'm going to sit on it and make sure it's comfort all the way."

Andy high-fived him. "Nice! And maybe bring in a different decorator. We all love Mom, but I think you might need to have a place that represents you better. That flowered pillow? It's got to go."

Noah laughed. "She snuck that one in on me."

As Noah put all of his clothes in one of the boxes his brothers had brought, his thoughts turned to Rachel. Was it possible that his brothers were right? A little glimmer of hope flickered in his heart. He hadn't realized how important she'd become when she was here because she was always present. And then she wasn't.

Adam taped up a box. "Men don't get all love-talkish very often. But as the married brother, I feel like I should ask this question because I've been there. I *am* there. Do you love her, Noah?"

The truth whooshed in. He felt like crying, but that wasn't something he was going to show to anyone, even a brother. He stared down into a half-filled box, thinking about the question. Did he have an answer? Could he dare to consider a future with her? Hurt and pain more deep than he'd already experienced could lie on that path.

"I think I might," he said the words slowly.

"I learned myself that whether or not you say the words or even think them, it's the same emotion inside of you." Adam patted his brother on the arm, then bent down to pick up the box.

"Yeah. I do love Rachel."

Adam stood with the box in his arms. "Then reach out to her. Don't let her get away." As he turned toward the door, he added, "And don't let Mom choose your bedding either."

Noah laughed. This had been the best evening he'd had in a long time.

~

Rachel peered through the windows of the storefront. Three long weeks of searching had netted her this. One more shop that wouldn't be right.

She stepped back to get a better look at it and turned in a circle to check out the stores on either side, across the street, and at the street itself. She'd shopped here many times. In fact, one of her favorite coffee shops was about a block down the road. There was a lot of foot traffic passing her on the sidewalk. She stopped to face the shop itself again. The rent was a little higher than she'd hoped to pay, but not overly so.

Her phone rang. Taking it out of her purse, she expected to have the phone say David was calling. He talked to her several times a week since she's gotten back from her trip. It was good to have a solid relationship with her brother now that they both understood each other and any differences that she'd perceived because of Fitzpatrick's had been pushed to the side.

Instead of his picture, Holly's face stared at her from her phone. She answered.

"Rachel?" Holly continued before she had a chance to say anything. "We miss you up here."

With Holly, she'd felt a connection that you rarely do with someone. A bond of instant friendship. Only this friend lived thousands of miles away.

"I'm fine. I'm standing in front of a possible storefront for my clothing store." She forced a perky town tone into her voice.

Holly paused for a moment before continuing. "So you settled down there and are making a new life?"

Had she? "My life from the moment I got here has been hectic."

"We all thought it would be, so we didn't want to bother you. But I read online that the transfer of the store was complete, so I thought I could call now."

The O'Connells had been following her that closely? Instead of feeling weird, that felt comforting. "Thank you. We wrapped up the final pieces of paperwork at the end of last week. I'm a free woman now." She forced more cheerfulness into her voice. Maybe if she kept doing that, it would sink into her soul, and she'd actually believe it.

"Is this the first shop you looked at?"

Rachel gave the storefront one last glance, then turned and started down the street. Maybe a cup of coffee at her favorite coffee shop would help calm her mind. "No, this is storefront number sixteen." She sighed. "They each had something wrong with them." Except this last one. It should have been perfect. What was wrong with it?

"I even called to check on one I'd seen in Anchorage just so I'd know what the terms should be for a lease and how many square feet it was." Because it had seemed perfect.

Holly hesitated again. "How are you doing without Noah?"

Rachel felt like a bomb had gone off inside her at the question. How did she feel without Noah? Instead of thinking the words for the thousandth time, she decided to speak them out loud. Maybe that would help purge her of this. "Holly, I am ripped apart. I miss him so much. I know that sounds crazy because I only knew him for a little over one week. But . . ."

As her words trailed away, the tears started. Again. She sat on one of the many benches that lined the street to pull herself together. Tugging out the packet of tissues that she'd learned to keep handy, she dabbed at her eyes, not wanting to smear makeup all over her face.

"I hoped you'd say that."

That pulled Rachel out of her thoughts. "You hoped I was in deep distress?"

"Rachel," Holly said in a softer tone. "I think Noah might feel the same way."

"What!" Rachel sprang to her feet. "And he hasn't contacted me?"

"Not at all?"

Rachel marched down the street toward her condo and privacy. "Well, yesterday I got a text from him asking if I'd accidentally taken his watch when I packed my bag. It's a weird thing to ask somebody a month later, you know?"

Holly chuckled.

"Not funny, Holly."

"Don't hang up on me, but it actually is. I think he might

be trying to communicate with you, but he doesn't know how."

Rachel stopped on the sidewalk. People had to move around her, and one man glanced back at her with a nasty expression. "All he has to do is pick up the phone." She said every word very deliberately.

"A woman would do that, right? We pick up the phone when we have any questions. We aren't afraid to speak." Holly said the same words that were rushing through Rachel's mind. "But he's a man, Rachel, they don't know how to do this."

Rachel pursed her lips. She continued walking as she thought about that. "You're married, Holly. And you probably dated before Adam."

"I was married before Adam. My first husband left me. I've learned a thing or two about how to talk to men."

She'd forgotten that. She stopped walking, but this time stepped to the side in front of a store. "What should I do?"

"Let me ask this question. Do you want Noah? I know you have a life where you are. But that's not the place for him. At least not at this time in his life."

Rachel took in the street and the things that were familiar. Then she thought about Alaska. She'd seen it at its best and maybe at its worst. "I'm a city girl, Holly. But Anchorage seems to have anything I could want."

"That's true. But it won't have your family or friends."

Rachel gave a wry laugh. "The moment the transfer was complete, my parents announced they were taking an around-the-world cruise. Neither of them said anything about hoping I did well in life now that the store was gone. They didn't even ask about my plans. They took away my livelihood, the only thing I'd known for work as long as I've been aware of such a thing, and they didn't once ask what I was going to do. They could have gotten me a job very easily in a similar business with someone they knew. One phone call and I would have at least had an interview."

Holly made a soft sound of sympathy. "I'm sorry, Rachel. I can't imagine that. Jemma and Bree and I have been blessed with loving parents. I married into a family where everyone is kind to each other. They aren't all alike, none of us are, but they accept that. I feel very loved and blessed."

At that moment, Rachel realized that Virginia and her condo only felt like home because she'd lived here all her life. It was familiar. But she'd made it familiar over time after she'd left her parents' house. She could make somewhere else familiar too. Somewhere that had instantly pulled her in with its magnetic appeal.

"Holly, you're right. There isn't anything for me here. At least nothing I can't recreate somewhere else." As Rachel looked across the street at the coffee shop, she thought of the Kobuk, the cute coffee shop she'd found in downtown Anchorage. She could do this. She could create a new life. With or without Noah. She would have David nearby, and they were already well on their way to building a relationship that overcame their earlier years.

This time when she continued toward her condo, every step carried purpose. Her surroundings blurred as she focused on plans for the future. "I'm coming to Alaska."

"Oh, that's great! How long will you be staying?"

"I'm not coming to visit, Holly. I am packing up, loading everything in my car, and moving to Alaska."

Holly gasped, sounding excited. "I didn't think you had a car."

"I bought one when I came back. I learned that a car gave

me freedom, and I felt like I needed that." She'd driven into the countryside the other day to see what it felt like away from the city. She hadn't minded it. Once she'd experienced the Alaskan wilderness, everywhere else seemed like a pretty easy place to live. And she found that the silence away from big cities could be a good thing.

"So, are you going to contact Noah?"

"Holly, he's the one that ended everything with his words. I think I need him to do better than asking about his watch. My guess is that it's on his wrist."

"Probably. But give him a chance." With that, they ended the call.

Rachel walked into her building and went to her unit. As she did, she considered what she would take with her and immediately decided to only bring what would fit in her car. And maybe she'd get a pet when she arrived in Alaska. It might be fun to have a dog like Zeke.

When she stepped out of the elevator doors, her elderly neighbor Mrs. Martino popped out of her unit.

"I heard the elevator and hoped it would be you, dear. My niece accepted a legal position off the Beltway and would like to live somewhere out here. Please keep your ear open for something good. I want her to be in a safe place."

Rachel's plans were so new. Could she break her ties to Virginia this easily? Yes. "Mrs. Martino, I'm moving. I could lease my apartment to her instead of selling it."

The older woman put her hand on her chest. "I'll miss you for sure, but that would be wonderful. I know that you fixed up your unit, and it's beautiful."

Rachel thought over all the furniture she was going to have to get rid of. "Since your niece recently graduated, she may not have a lot of furniture. Am I right?"

"She's been a typical frugal college student, my dear, and lived in a shared, furnished apartment with three other law students. I've been looking forward to shopping with her when she gets here."

Rachel put the key into her door and opened it. "Why don't you come in and take pictures now, Mrs. Martino, before I pack everything up. Then your niece—what's her name?"

"Sandy."

"Sandy can see if this would suit her. I won't take any of my furniture, so she's welcome to use it."

While Rachel made a list of everything she did want to take, her neighbor snapped photos of the apartment with her phone. She heard voices from her master bedroom and hoped that the older woman was not talking to herself.

Mrs. Martino walked out to the kitchen. "I sent the photos to Sandy, and she wants this place. She did mention something about being too close to relatives." The older woman chuckled. "That may be true. But she loved what she saw, and the location is ideal."

"Then have her contact me. I'll be out of here within the week."

When she was once again alone in her condo, Rachel gave it a long look. She'd been comfortable here. But she could easily make another place feel this good.

CHAPTER TWENTY

*D*riving past a sign that said she was leaving Virginia and one welcoming her to Maryland made Rachel's journey seem very real. She was on the other side of the country from Alaska. This would be a long drive.

Flickers of panic trickled in. She pushed them away. She could do this. She'd be fine. Holly had asked her to check in regularly, and she would, as soon as she got to tonight's destination, which she'd plotted on the map as just outside of Cleveland, Ohio. It had been a late start. For right now, she'd enjoy the scenery going by and explore America on her way to her new home.

Noah's face kept popping into her mind. She felt his arms around her both in comfort and more than that. Since her talk with Holly, she'd reached out to Noah with a simple question of how he was doing. She hadn't known whether or not she'd receive a reply. In typical male fashion, at least in this male's typical fashion, his reply had been somewhat elusive.

I'm okay, he'd texted. *I'm temporarily at Adam and Holly's house.*

It seemed like an odd place to be living, and why was he temporarily there? She hoped he was okay.

About dinnertime, she pulled into the hotel she had booked for the night. As soon as she was settled, she gave Holly a call.

"Rachel! I was just thinking of you. How's the packing going?"

"The packing *went* fine."

Silence greeted her. "Does that mean you changed your mind?"

Rachel laughed at that idea. "I have signed the lease for the storefront in Anchorage for my business and have three apartments ready to tour the moment I arrive there. Everything I own is either back in my condo and leased to my neighbor's niece, or it's in my car. There's no turning back now, Holly."

A gleeful sound came through her phone. "So you're actually coming?" Holly sounded as excited as one of her girls would, and that warmed Rachel's heart. It was good to have a friend waiting for her on the other end.

"I'm in a hotel on the outskirts of Cleveland. A full day's drive tomorrow should get me to Wisconsin. I have a reservation in a hotel there, so I hope my planning is good. I've obviously never done this before."

Rachel could hear the laughter in Holly's voice when she said, "You've made reservations for every night along the way, haven't you? Everything's planned?"

"I'm so used to planning everything in business that it didn't occur to me to be spontaneous."

But she had been spontaneous with Noah. She kind of

liked that. Maybe she'd have to adopt that lifestyle permanently or at least try it more.

She heard a male voice near Holly. "Adam says he wants
to make sure you're okay. Text your itinerary when we get
off the phone so we'll know where you should be each night.
Is that too pushy?"

Rachel enjoyed the fact that someone cared if she was
alive or not. "Not too pushy. I'll get it to you after I find
something for dinner around here. Probably fast food, but I
hope not since lunch was too."

"You're not used to car trips, so you don't have a lifetime
of tricks up your sleeve. In the morning, get yourself an ice
chest—any of the discount stores will have one—put some
ice in it, then add drinks and snacks and things like that so
you have what you need while you're driving."

"That's easy. And I know I've seen that on movies and TV.
I feel kind of like an idiot for not even considering that. I
should have researched road trips before I did this."

Holly laughed. "Rachel, people don't always research
everything before they do it. Go with the flow. Maybe good
things will happen along the way."

Should she ask about Noah living with her and Adam?
Doing that felt like she would be intruding on his life too
much, and Holly hadn't mentioned it. She would learn what
had happened when she arrived in Anchorage. Rachel
yawned. "It's been a long day. I finished packing around
dawn. Then I had someone I knew from Fitzpatrick's help
me load everything into my car, and I drove for hours. I
think I'd better get something to eat before I fall asleep."

After they hung up, Rachel did as she'd said. When she
came back to her room after her fast food dinner, which

truly was the only thing around, she fell asleep the second she laid down.

On her third day of travel, Rachel stopped at the scheduled hotel in North Dakota. She'd left Wisconsin early, so it was mid-afternoon, but she'd be crossing into Canada tomorrow, and she wanted to make sure she had plenty of time to take care of that and still be able to get some driving in that day. With her overnight bag slung over her shoulder, she went into the hotel.

As the doors slid open, a man rose from a chair in the lobby. He looked exactly like Noah. But that couldn't be. She took a step closer to him.

"Rachel, it's good to see you." He moved one foot as though he was going to take a step forward, then set it back down.

She dropped her bag on the floor and ran toward him with her arms outstretched. "Noah!"

He held out his arms when she was halfway there and stepped forward to meet her, pulling her tightly to him as soon as they reached each other. Neither one of them moved. They just held on tightly.

Against his shoulder, she said, "Noah, I'm supposed to be here. But why are *you* here?" She stepped back.

Noah glanced over at the front desk, and she followed his glance. The woman working there was watching them as though she was watching a movie.

"Why don't I check in, and then you can talk to me in my room where it's more private," she whispered the last words.

In her room a few minutes later, she sat on the edge of the bed, and he sat on the chair at the desk.

"You asked me why I'm here, Rachel. I came to see you."

She fought the tears that tried to come. She would not cry

over this man again. "Noah, you made yourself very clear. You told me I was no longer needed in Alaska. So why do you want to see me now?"

He looked down, then back up at her with a pained expression. "I wanted you to do everything you wanted. I didn't want to stand in your way. You like big cities, and you wanted to have your store in Virginia. I couldn't say that I wanted you to be in Alaska. That would be wrong."

"What changed?"

He stood, walked over to the window, then turned and faced her. "I've been told that I made a mistake. When Mom found out, she told me I was stupid."

Rachel grinned at that. Then she realized what he might be saying. "Are you saying that you cared about me and wanted me to stay?" Did she dare even hope that?

"Rachel, I want to spend every day of my life with you. You're joy, you're laughter, you're everything I could want in a life partner."

He dropped to one knee in front of her, reached into his pocket, pulled out a jewelry box, and opened it. A simple but elegant diamond engagement and wedding ring set sparkled in the box. "We may have gotten married too soon the last time, so I think we should plan a wedding later in the year, don't you?"

Rachel stared at the rings in the box. With a shaking hand, she reached forward and took them out to try them on her finger. They fit.

"I went to the same jewelry store we used for the other ring, and they knew your size. But enough about jewelry, Rachel, will you marry me? For real this time. Forever this time."

As she leaned forward, he met her halfway for the kiss

that she had been wanting since the last one months ago. "Noah O'Connell, I will marry you this time for real. This time forever." After the kiss, she sighed.

Then the fact that he was in North Dakota made her pause. How had he gotten here? "Did you fly your plane all the way here?" Without waiting for an answer, she said, "We're in a hotel room in North Dakota, nowhere near Alaska, and I have a car. We can't fly out of here together."

He held her hand. "It's okay. Colton's back from leave and Sarah's vacation is over. I'm on vacation, and I flew commercial planes to get here today. I'm planning to finish the drive with you, if you'd like."

She leaned her forehead against his. "I would love that. But I think we may have to go to the post office first thing in the morning and mail a box of my things to Alaska. You aren't going to fit in the car right now."

He chuckled. "Lots of stuff?"

"I didn't ship anything. It's all in my car." A moment later, she added, "My store will be in Anchorage, Noah, not Kenai. Is that okay with you?"

"I need to live in Anchorage for work, and I'm learning to enjoy city life. You can help me choose a new apartment. The last one didn't turn out too well."

She smiled. "Maybe we can choose an apartment that we'll both love after we're married." Then she leaned forward and kissed him.

BONUS EPILOGUE

*H*olly and her sisters Jemma and Bree watched from the sidelines at the O'Connell family picnic just outside of Kenai. People paired off so that Adam could tie their inside legs together for a three-legged race.

Jemma bounced her daughter in her arms. "Noah and Rachel make such a cute couple. Their race challenge is that they won't be able to stare into each other's eyes while they're racing."

Holly laughed. "They are a great couple."

Jemma added. "And you helped bring them together."

"I did. Mrs. O'Connell believes she's the matchmaker." They all turned toward the elder Mrs. O'Connell. She wore a satisfied expression as she watched her son and his new fiancée.

"But you stepped in and saved the match."

Holly nodded. "I could tell they belonged together right away. Rachel and I are becoming good friends and having Noah at our house made the matchmaking even easier. They both knew what they wanted. I just gave them a nudge."

As Adam walked over to the sidelines to start the race, Holly's twin girls, their legs tied together, bounced with excitement.

Bree sighed and rubbed her very pregnant belly. "Your family events get bigger and bigger. I'm glad we're invited, even if we aren't O'Connells."

"They're nice people. *We're* nice people. I'm an O'Connell." She grinned. "Rachel will also be glad she married into this family."

Holly said, "The group grew larger when you married Adam, then Jemma had her daughter, and you'll have your baby soon, whatever his or her name is. . ."

Bree grinned. "We have names chosen either way. You'll learn after the birth."

Jemma pointed straight ahead. "Noah and Rachel are holding hands at the starting line."

Adam shouted, "Go," and the race began.

"Noah and Rachel are in the lead! Go!" Jemma called out. Then she winced when they tripped and hit the ground. "At least they were. But they're laughing even while lying in the dirt."

Holly pointed at her girls. "They won!"

Bree started walking toward a picnic table. "Abbie and Ivy were the youngest and fastest. I need to sit down. I'm looking forward to moving swifter than a waddle again."

Jemma and Holly walked with her. They sat on a bench at a currently unoccupied table.

"I've been watching everyone." Jemma turned to her sisters. "What's your take on Mark?"

Holly shook her head. "He's the oldest of the brothers. He clearly loves his family. But he seems lonely and a little sad at times."

Jemma gave a satisfied nod. "That's exactly what I thought."

Holly quickly put her hand on her sister's arm. "Jemma, I think he has baggage from the past. His mother says he lived alone in a log cabin in the woods in Colorado. He sounds like he might have been a hermit, but I don't know why."

Jemma watched Mark talk and laugh with his brothers. "He came back to Alaska, though. That shows he's ready to be part of the family again, don't you think?"

Bree nodded. "I agree about that. But I don't know if that means he's ready for romance."

Holly's gaze moved from Mark over to his brother Noah and his new fiancée. When she looked back at Mark, he was also watching his brother as Noah put his arm around his fiancée. Mark had an expression on his face that she would have to peg as longing. "You may be right that he's lonely."

"I believe so."

"Are you playing matchmaker, Jemma?"

Jemma nodded slowly. "I think I am. But *only* if I find the right woman for him."

Bree said, "What about the other two O'Connell brothers, Jack and Andy? Nice, handsome, and intelligent men should have wives, shouldn't they?"

"Are you saying you want to be a matchmaker too?"

Bree watched the picnic. "I think I'd be a good matchmaker. But it may need to be after the baby's born." She patted her belly. "I'll have to think about which one of the brothers to choose to help."

Holly chuckled. "Will they consider you a helper?"

Bree grinned. "Maybe not at first."

Jemma focused on the oldest O'Connell. "I'm watching Mark for clues for his right match."

Holly nudged her sister. "Try not to be so obvious. Why don't you look away before he gets suspicious, and I'll give you updates." A moment later, she continued, "He turned away from the crowd and went back to the food table and straight to the dessert section. Maybe a woman who likes to bake would be right for him."

Jemma turned toward Mark again. "Something about him makes me think he wants to be happy."

Holly also wanted to see her brother-in-law happy. "I don't know who the right woman would be for Mark O'Connell."

"Don't warn him, but I'm officially looking for her."

"Should I ask Adam if he thinks his brother would be interested in a match? My husband is close to all of his brothers."

Jemma turned toward Holly. "I think you should wait until I have my sights on someone."

"That makes sense. Once you do, I can check to make sure Adam's okay with your meddling."

Jemma's eyebrows rose. "Meddling?"

"Do you believe that matchmaking is anything but meddling?"

Jemma watched Mark walk over to Noah and Rachel. "I'd prefer to think of it as making two people happy."

Holly grinned. "Then let the happiness begin."

WHAT'S NEXT?

Noah's brother Mark is the next O'Connell to meet his match. Well, he actually already knows her. Mark and Maddie were engaged when they were teenagers, but she broke it off. They're getting their second chance for love in *Finally Matched*.

I loved David and Katie so much that I wrote a FREE short story about when they met and the proposal. Get *Quickly Matched* at cathrynbrown.com/quickly.

WHAT'S AFTER THAT?

Each of the O'Connell brothers meet their match in the Alaska Matchmakers Romance series. But matchmakers Jemma, Bree, and Holly met their husbands in the Alaska Dream Romance series. If you haven't read them yet, you don't want to miss *Falling for Alaska* (Jemma's story), *Loving Alaska* (Bree's story), and *Crazy About Alaska*, (Holly and Adam's story).

ABOUT CATHRYN

Writing books that are fun and touch your heart

Even though Cathryn Brown always loved to read, she didn't plan to be a writer. She earned two degrees from the University of Alaska, one in journalism/public communications, but didn't become a journalist.

Years passed. Cathryn felt pulled into a writing life, testing her wings with a novel and moving on to articles. She's now an award-winning journalist who has sold hundreds articles to local, national, and regional publications.

The Feather Chase, written as Shannon L. Brown, was her first published book and begins the Crime-Solving Cousins Mystery series. The eight-to-twelve-year-olds in your life will enjoy this contemporary twist on a Nancy Drew–type mystery.

Cathryn enjoys hiking, sometimes while dictating a book. She also unwinds by baking and reading.

Cathryn lives in Nashville, Tennessee, with her professor husband and adorable calico cat.

Made in the USA
Las Vegas, NV
12 December 2021

37363645R00121